Introduction to Ramayana

A Different Perspective

Melody of Unknown and Untold

Aurobindo Ghosh

Ukiyoto Publishing

DEDICATION

I dedicate this book to my mentors and my school teachers of Durgacharan High School, Bhagalpur, Bihar. I can't resist myself from expressing my deep sense of gratitude to my Headmaster Gurudasbabu, Sanatbabu, Binoybabu, Siddhibabu and college teachers Lohitda, Keshtoda, Jituda and others who shaped my life.

My heartfelt gratitude goes to my wife, Dr. Sharada Ghosh, who's discerning eye and unwavering commitment to excellence have been invaluable to this book. As a dedicated critic and meticulous editor, she has not only identified every flaw but has also painstakingly worked to make each story flow seamlessly. Her tireless efforts in editing, compiling, and organizing these narratives have been essential to this work.

I am also profoundly grateful to my children Dr. Dorothy, Dr. Gargi, and Aalap who form the foundation of my support system. Their encouragement and faith in my writing give me the strength to pursue this passion. To each of you, thank you for your patience, understanding, and belief in me.

Lastly, let me take this opportunity to convey my gratitude to all the team members of Ukiyoto publishing for their maximum care to make this book a magnificent creation.

Contents

Foreword

I know my brother Dr. Aurobindo Ghosh since his birth. He belongs to a renowned Mahashayjee family of Bhagalpur. His multifaceted talent was visible in his early age. In academic field, he completed his B.Sc, M.Sc, M.Phil, Ph.D in Economics, Ph.D in Statistics. As a college professor, he was always in demand. In social field, his contribution to the society is unparallel. He collected quite a few Good Samaritan to perform marriage to quite a few poor marriageable girls in Amravati, Maharashtra. His linguistic ability is notable. He can speak, read and write in Bengali, Hindi, Marathi, Bhagalpuri, English, and Gujarati with ease. His passion for writing in various languages resulted in many solo and anthologies. Notable amongst them are Lily on the Northern Sky (Awarded by Ukiyoto), Insight Outsight (A collection of short stories), Mejoder Golpo (Bengali short story collection), Chhondo Hole Mondo Ki (Bengali Poems), Bimladadi's Dream (Awarded by Ukiyoto), Mystical Honeymoon, and Deception Redefined. Recently he has introduced his detective character Suborno Deb Barman through his trilogy, "Mysteries of Suborno Deb barman (14 crime stories), Chronicles of Suborno Deb Barman (Six crime stories) and Chronicles of Suborno Deb Barman-Mystery of stolen memory". His short stories and poems in different languages are included in more than twenty anthologies. Many of his books are translated in various international languages such as German, Italian, Spanish, Turkish, French, and Nepali and so on. He is also an artist of high caliber.

He is expert in Madhubani and Warli painting. His acrylic abstracts are appreciated a lot. He is a traveler who travels around the globe. Recently he has shifted his attention towards Mythological research in Indian context. His critical analytical book on Mahabharata is coming soon. This present book on Ramayana is the natural extension of the first one.

The Ramayana, an epic that has stood the test of time, transcends its role as a mere narrative of Lord Rama's journey. It is a rich tapestry of themes, characters, and values that speak to the essence of human existence, offering insights that resonate far beyond the confines of religion, geography, or era. Rooted in the principles of dharma (righteousness), karuna (compassion), tyaga (sacrifice), and satya (truth), the Ramayana continues to be a cornerstone of philosophical and ethical discourse, a guide for individuals and societies alike. Despite its grand narrative, many facets of the Ramayana remain underexplored. While the heroics of Rama, Sita, Lakshmana, and Hanuman have captured the collective imagination, the epic's depth is enriched by the seemingly minor characters and subplots that weave through its vast expanse. These often-overlooked elements carry profound lessons, embodying virtues and dilemmas that are as relevant today as they were in the past. This book, *Ramayana: A Different Perspective*, seeks to shine a light on these hidden dimensions, offering readers a fresh lens to view the epic and uncover its boundless wisdom.

This book is not only in its grand arcs but also in its intricate nuances. Characters such journey of this book begins with the realization that the Ramayana's strength lies as Shabari, Jatayu, Vibhisana, and Mandodari, though peripheral to the main story, leave an indelible mark. Shabari's unwavering devotion teaches us the power of faith and simplicity. Jatayu's valor and sacrifice exemplify selflessness and loyalty. Bibhishan's steadfastness in choosing dharma over familial ties highlights the courage required to stand for righteousness. Mandodari's resilience and wisdom reveal the quiet strength of a woman often overshadowed by her circumstances. These figures, among others, form the moral backbone of the epic, reminding us that greatness often lies in the unnoticed corners of a narrative.

Brotherhood emerges as one of the central themes of the Ramayana, exemplified in the relationships between Rama, Lakshmana, Bharata, and Shatrughna. Each brother's actions reflect love, loyalty, and sacrifice, underscoring the importance of familial unity in overcoming life's adversities. Bharata's refusal to ascend the throne during Rama's exile is a testament to his humility and reverence for dharma. Lakshmana's unwavering support for Rama highlights the strength of bonds forged in shared purpose and duty. These relationships resonate deeply, offering timeless lessons on leadership, unity, and resilience. Another pivotal theme is the tension between duty and personal desire. The Ramayana delves into the struggles of balancing governance with personal relationships and the pursuit of dharma amidst complex human emotions. For instance, Rama's adherence to his father's promise, even at great personal cost, is a profound exploration of duty over desire. Similarly, Sita's trials illuminate the endurance required to uphold dignity and truth in the face of adversity. These moral dilemmas challenge readers to reflect on their values and choices, making the Ramayana a mirror for our own lives.

The relevance of the Ramayana to the modern world cannot be overstated. As societies grapple with the complexities of relationships, leadership, and ethical decision-making, the epic offers a timeless roadmap. It advocates for compassionate leadership, grounded in integrity and empathy, as seen in Rama's governance of Ayodhya. In a world often marred by division, the Ramayana's emphasis on unity, resilience, and the pursuit of collective good provides a guiding light. The Ramayana's universality is another facet explored in this book. While deeply rooted in Indian culture, its narrative transcends national boundaries, echoing across Southeast Asia in diverse art forms, rituals, and cultural expressions. From the Ramakien in Thailand to the Hikayat Seri Rama in Malaysia, the tale of Rama has been adapted and re-imagined, reflecting the shared values and heritage of humanity. This global appeal underscores the epic's ability to connect with people from varied backgrounds, reaffirming its position as a timeless and universal text.

One of the most profound aspects of the Ramayana is its portrayal of Rama as both divine and human. While celebrated as an avatar of Vishnu, Rama's humanity is what makes him relatable. His struggles, triumphs, and choices reflect the complexities of human existence, offering a blueprint for living a life anchored in dharma. This duality invites readers to see the Ramayana not just as a tale of divine intervention but as a story of human experiences and struggles. This book also delves into the nuanced relationships that enrich the Ramayana. The bond between Rama and Hanuman, built on mutual respect and devotion, illustrates the power of service and friendship. The loyalty of Sugriva and the valor of Angada reveal the strength of alliances forged in shared purpose. Even Ravana, the epic's antagonist, is portrayed with complexity, his virtues and flaws offering insights into the consequences of unchecked ambition and desire. By examining these relationships, *Ramayana: A Different Perspective* provides a holistic view of the epic, celebrating its intricate emotional and moral tapestry.

The Ramayana's exploration of gender roles is another area of reflection. Characters like Sita, Mandodari, and Kaikeyi are not mere participants but active agents whose decisions shape the narrative. Sita's strength lies in her unwavering commitment to dharma, even in the face of immense trials. Kaikeyi's actions, though controversial, highlight the complexities of human motives and relationships. Mandodari's wisdom and resilience offer a counterpoint to the ambition and pride of her husband, Ravana. By bringing these perspectives to the forefront, this book seeks to enrich our understanding of the epic's depth and diversity. In examining the Ramayana's lesser-known characters and themes, this work also seeks to bridge the past and the present. It emphasizes the epic's relevance in addressing contemporary issues such as ethical leadership, the balance between personal and professional responsibilities, and the pursuit of justice and harmony. The timeless values of the Ramayana serve as a guide for navigating the complexities of modern life, reminding us of the enduring power of dharma and compassion.

Through its exploration of these dimensions, *Ramayana: A Different Perspective* invites readers on a journey of rediscovery. It challenges them to look beyond the surface and engage with the epic's profound wisdom. Whether one approaches the Ramayana as a spiritual text, a work of literature, or a historical document, its lessons remain universally applicable, offering insights into the human condition and the pursuit of a meaningful life. For scholars and casual readers alike, this book promises an enlightening experience. It is an invitation to revisit an ancient tale, to uncover its hidden layers, and to draw inspiration from its timeless truths. In doing so, it reaffirms the Ramayana's place not just as a relic of the past but as a living document of human values and aspirations. As you embark on this journey through *Ramayana: A Different Perspective*, may you find new insights, renewed inspiration, and a deeper connection to the timeless wisdom of this epic. Let the stories of devotion, sacrifice, and resilience guide you, and let the lessons of the Ramayana illuminate your path, reminding us all of the enduring power of righteousness, compassion, and truth.

Sulata Sinha, Mythologist,
Ex-Principal, Indian Community School,
Benghazi, Libya, Traveler and book critic
Kolkata, 10/12/2024

Preface

The Ramayana, an epic that has stood the test of time, is much more than a story of Lord Rama's journey. It is a rich tapestry of themes, characters, and values that transcend the boundaries of religion, geography, and culture. This magnificent epic offers profound lessons not only for individuals but also for societies, making it eternally relevant. Its teachings resonate with timeless values dharma (righteousness), karuna (compassion), tyaga (sacrifice), and satya (truth) making it a cornerstone of philosophical and ethical discourse.

However, amidst the grandeur of this epic, many significant aspects remain overshadowed. The limelight is often focused on the heroics of the central characters, leaving in its shadows a treasure trove of lesser-known stories and personalities. Yet, these seemingly minor characters and subtle themes play a vital role in shaping the narrative and imparting invaluable lessons. It is this uncharted dimension of the Ramayana that forms the core of Ramayana: A Different Perspective.

This book is an attempt to shift the lens, to uncover the hidden layers of the epic, and to provide a fresh perspective on the vastness of its wisdom. It focuses on characters that, despite their apparent insignificance in the grand scheme, leave a lasting impact on the epic's moral and emotional framework. Be it the unwavering devotion of Shabari, the valor and loyalty of Jatayu, the humility of Vibhisana, or the resilience of Mandodari, each of these figures exemplifies virtues that continue to inspire. Their actions, though often overlooked, form the moral bedrock of the Ramayana.

In addition to exploring these overlooked characters, the book delves into the intricate themes that flow seamlessly through the epic. Brotherhood, for instance, emerges as a cornerstone of the Ramayana, beautifully exemplified through the relationships of Rama, Lakshmana, Bharata, and Shatrughna. The dynamics of their bonds rooted in love, loyalty, and sacrifice offer lessons on unity and the strength of family in the face of adversity.

The theme of duty versus personal desires also occupies a pivotal space in this exploration. How does a ruler balance the demands of governance with personal relationships? How does one reconcile the path of dharma with the complexities of human emotions? The Ramayana addresses these questions, often presenting characters caught in the web of moral dilemmas, their choices defining their legacies.

This book also highlights the Ramayana's relevance to the modern world. Despite being an ancient text, its teachings are universal and timeless. In an age marked by growing complexities in relationships, leadership challenges, and societal changes, the Ramayana offers a roadmap for ethical living, compassionate leadership, and resilience in the face of adversity. It shows how adherence to values can guide nations and individuals toward harmony and progress, proving that the epic is not merely a relic of the past but a living document of life's eternal truths.

Another significant focus of this work is the exploration of how the Ramayana transcends national and cultural boundaries. The tale of Rama is not confined to India but echoes across Southeast Asia, with its themes adapted into diverse art forms, rituals, and cultural expressions. This universality speaks to the enduring appeal of its values, reminding us of the shared heritage of humanity.

Finally, this book challenges readers to view the Ramayana not just as a tale of divine intervention but as a story of human experiences and struggles. It portrays Rama as a human with divine qualities, grappling with challenges that test his character, and shows how his responses serve as a blueprint for leading a life rooted in dharma.

Through its exploration of insignificant characters, thematic reviews, and contemporary relevance, Ramayana: A Different Perspective aims to reignite interest in this epic while offering a fresh lens for its interpretation. It invites readers to go beyond the surface and delve deeper into the intricacies of the Ramayana, uncovering its profound wisdom and understanding its relevance in today's world.

For those who seek to see the Ramayana in a new light, for scholars and casual readers alike, this book promises an enlightening journey through the less-trodden paths of this timeless epic. It is an invitation to revisit an ancient tale and discover its boundless potential to inspire and guide humanity, even in the modern era.

Chapter One Origination of the name 'Ramayana' and its Kandas

The word Ramayana is derived from two Sanskrit components: Rama and Ayana. To understand the full meaning and evolution of the name, let's break it down:

1. Rama:

•	Rama is the central figure of the epic. He is considered the seventh incarnation (avatar) of Lord Vishnu, one of the principal deities of the Hindu trinity (Brahma, Vishnu, Shiva).

•	Rama is depicted as the ideal man, a prince who embodies virtue, honor, duty (dharma), bravery, and devotion. He is known for his unwavering commitment to righteousness and his willingness to sacrifice personal desires for the greater good.

2. Ayana:

•	Ayana is a Sanskrit word that means "path," "journey," or "way." It refers to a course or a path that one follows, often in the context of a journey in life or a divine mission.

•	In some interpretations, Ayana can also mean "coming" or "movement," signifying a journey or a progression towards a goal or destination.

3. Combined Meaning - Ramayana:

• When combined, Ramayana literally translates to "The Journey of Rama" or "The Path of Rama." The title reflects the epic's central theme: the life journey of Lord Rama, which encompasses his birth, exile, the abduction of his wife Sita, his battle against the demon king Ravana, and ultimately his return to his kingdom.

• More than just a physical journey, the Ramayana also represents the spiritual and moral journey of Rama, who traverses various challenges and trials to uphold dharma (righteousness), fulfill his duties, and ultimately achieve victory over evil.

4. Evolution of the Name:

• The term Ramayana is thought to have evolved during the time the epic was passed down through generations. Though attributed to the sage Valmiki, who is said to have composed the Ramayana in Sanskrit, the story of Rama existed in various oral traditions and versions even before it was written down.

• Valmiki's epic is considered the oldest and most authoritative text on the life of Rama, and over time, the name "Ramayana" became synonymous with the story of Lord Rama. The title highlights not just the sequence of events but also the moral and ethical lessons that Rama's life and actions impart to humanity.

• As the Ramayana spread across the Indian subcontinent and beyond, different versions of the epic emerged in various languages and cultures, each adding unique elements while retaining the central message of Rama's divine journey.

5. Symbolic Significance of the Name:

•   The name Ramayana not only describes the literal journey of Rama but also symbolizes the universal journey of life, filled with challenges, trials, and opportunities for spiritual growth. The epic teaches that one must follow the path of righteousness (dharma) as demonstrated by Rama, regardless of the obstacles faced, whether they be personal, familial, or societal.

•   The Ramayana thus serves as both a historical narrative and a spiritual guide, showing how an ideal human being navigates the complexities of life with honor, integrity, and devotion to duty.

In essence, the name Ramayana encapsulates the timeless and profound story of Rama's life, his adherence to dharma, and his quest to restore cosmic order by vanquishing evil, which resonates with readers and followers of the epic across generations and cultures.

Analytical explanation of Each Kanda in the Ramayana

The Ramayana, a timeless epic by Valmiki, captures the essence of life's highest ideals. Each Kanda (section) is a crucial phase in Lord Rama's journey and holds significant teachings.

1. Balakanda (The Childhood Section)

The Balakanda introduces the story of Rama's divine birth and his formative years. King Dasharatha, childless despite his three queens, performs the Putrakameshti Yajna. Lord Vishnu incarnates as Rama to defeat the demon king Ravana, while Lakshmana, Bharata, and Shatrughna accompany him as his brothers.

As a young prince, Rama trains under Sage Vishwamitra, learning divine knowledge and weaponry. He demonstrates valor by killing the demoness Tataka and protecting the sage's sacrificial rites. Rama's heroic stringing of Shiva's bow in King Janaka's court earns him Sita's hand in marriage.

Teachings

- **Respect for Gurus**:

Rama's obedience to Sage Vishwamitra illustrates the profound respect that a disciple must have for their spiritual teacher. His unwavering respect for Vishwamitra, despite the challenges and dangers they face, teaches that knowledge and wisdom, particularly spiritual knowledge, are invaluable. It emphasizes the importance of humility in learning and the profound transformation that follows when one submits to a worthy teacher.

- **Use of Power for Good**:

Rama's victories over demons like Tataka highlight how true power should be used for the protection of the righteous and for upholding dharma (moral order). Rather than using his strength for personal gain, Rama consistently uses his abilities to help others, setting an example of selfless leadership and the importance of using one's strength for the greater good of society.

- **Marital Unity**:

The union of Rama and Sita is not just a love story; it represents an ideal marriage based on mutual respect, love, and duty. Their marriage teaches that love should not be based on superficial qualities but on deep emotional and moral compatibility, with both partners sharing the responsibility of supporting each other in fulfilling their duties, regardless of the hardships they may face.

2. Ayodhyakanda (The Ayodhya Section)

This Kanda reveals the strength of Rama's character as he sacrifices the throne for his stepmother Kaikeyi's wishes. Kaikeyi, manipulated by her maid Manthara, demands that her son Bharata be crowned king and Rama be exiled for 14 years. Despite the shock, Rama willingly accepts, upholding his father's honor.

Accompanied by Sita and Lakshmana, Rama leaves Ayodhya for the forest. Bharata, upon learning of

Kaikeyi's actions, refuses the throne and instead rules Ayodhya as a caretaker, placing Rama's sandals on the throne.

Teachings

- **Adherence to Dharma:**

Rama's decision to go into exile, even when it meant sacrificing his rightful throne, emphasizes the importance of following dharma, or righteous conduct, no matter the personal cost. His decision reflects the idea that upholding moral values and honoring promises is more important than personal ambition or wealth. This teaches that sometimes, one must make personal sacrifices for the greater good and to maintain societal harmony.

- **Brotherly Devotion:**

Bharata's refusal to accept the throne and his decision to place Rama's sandals on it demonstrate his deep devotion to his brother and his understanding that the kingdom belongs to Rama by right. His act teaches the value of loyalty, selflessness, and the importance of supporting one's family, even when personal interests are at stake. Bharata's actions also show that love for one's family should be rooted in sacrifice and duty.

- **Selflessness:**

Sita and Lakshmana's decision to accompany Rama into the forest, leaving behind the comforts of the palace, exemplifies the idea of unconditional love and selflessness. This act shows that true love is not just about companionship but about sharing the challenges and burdens that life may throw one's way. It teaches that selfless support for others is a cornerstone of any meaningful relationship.

3. Aranyakanda (The Forest Section)

During their exile, Rama, Sita, and Lakshmana encounter various sages and demons. Rama protects sages from the demons Khara, Dushana, and others, showcasing his duty as a guardian of dharma.

The demoness Surpanakha, enchanted by Rama's beauty, tries to seduce him but is humiliated by Lakshmana. In retaliation, her brothers attack but are defeated. Ravana, angered by this, abducts Sita with the help of the demon Maricha, who transforms into a golden deer to lure Rama away.

Teachings

- **Control over Desire:**

The episode with Surpanakha, who tries to seduce Rama and Lakshmana, demonstrates the need for self-control and the importance of maintaining one's moral integrity in the face of temptation. Both brothers resist her advances, teaching that true strength lies in the ability to control one's desires and focus on higher goals rather than being swayed by fleeting attractions.

- **Protection of Dharma:**

Rama's defense of the sages and his actions in protecting them from the demons illustrate the importance of upholding righteousness and protecting those who contribute positively to society. It shows that those who follow the path of dharma must protect it from forces that wish to disrupt peace and moral order. Rama's role as the protector of sages teaches the value of safeguarding wisdom and purity in a society.

- **Caution against Deception:**

Sita's abduction by Ravana, disguised as a golden deer, warns about the dangers of illusions and deceit. Ravana uses a distraction to lure Rama away from his dwelling, but the consequences of falling for such tricks are severe. This episode teaches the importance of discernment and caution, particularly when faced with seemingly attractive or ideal situations. It emphasizes that appearances can be deceiving, and one must be vigilant.

4. Kishkindhakanda (The Kishkindha Section)

This section focuses on Rama's alliance with Sugriva, the exiled monkey king of Kishkindha. Sugriva seeks Rama's help to defeat his brother Vali, who has usurped his throne. Rama kills Vali, restoring Sugriva's kingship. In return, Sugriva promises to help search for Sita.

Hanuman, a devoted servant of Sugriva, becomes Rama's greatest ally. The Vanaras (monkey warriors) begin their quest to locate Sita, led by Hanuman.

Teachings

- **The Power of Friendship**:

The alliance between Rama and Sugriva teaches that strong, mutually supportive relationships are essential for overcoming challenges. Despite their initial differences, both Rama and Sugriva support each other in times of need. Rama helps Sugriva regain his kingdom, and in return, Sugriva promises to help Rama find Sita. This teaches the value of cooperation and how genuine friendships can help individuals achieve their goals.

- **Righteous Action**:

Rama's killing of Vali, though controversial, is justified by his adherence to dharma, as Vali's actions were in opposition to righteousness. Rama's intervention teaches that sometimes difficult actions must be taken to protect the greater good. It emphasizes that actions must be guided by morality, even when they may be difficult or misunderstood by others.

- **Teamwork and Dedication**:

The Vanaras' dedicated search for Sita demonstrates the importance of teamwork. Hanuman's leadership and the collective effort of the monkey warriors highlight the strength that comes from working together. This teaches that collaboration, dedication, and mutual trust are powerful tools for solving even the most daunting problems.

5. Sundarakanda ('The Beautiful' Section)

The Sundarakanda is a tribute to Hanuman's devotion and heroism. Hanuman leaps across the ocean to Lanka, where he discovers Sita imprisoned in Ashoka Vatika. He reassures her of Rama's impending arrival and offers hope amidst her despair.

Hanuman demonstrates his power by burning Ravana's city when he is captured and insulted. His return to Rama with news of Sita marks the beginning of the preparations for the battle against Ravana.

Teachings

- **Unwavering Devotion:**

Hanuman's journey to Lanka showcases the strength of devotion. His single-minded determination to find Sita, despite facing numerous obstacles, teaches that unwavering faith and commitment can overcome even the most insurmountable odds. Hanuman's selflessness in serving Rama is a model of devotion and loyalty.

- **Courage in Adversity:**

Hanuman's actions, particularly when he is captured and humiliated by Ravana, demonstrate that courage is not the absence of fear, but the willingness to act in spite of it. His burning of Lanka is not just an act of revenge, but also a symbolic gesture of the triumph of good over evil. This episode teaches that true courage involves standing firm in the face of adversity and standing up for what is right.

- **Hope Amidst Despair**:

Hanuman's reassuring message to Sita, and his delivery of Rama's ring, offers her hope in her darkest hour. Hanuman's actions teach that hope can be a powerful motivator and that even in the most challenging times, support from others can make all the difference.

6. Yuddhakanda (The War Section)

The Yuddhakanda narrates the epic battle between Rama's forces and Ravana's army. Rama, with the help of the Vanaras, builds a bridge (Ram Setu) across the ocean to Lanka. The fierce battle sees the deaths of Ravana's sons, brothers, and ultimately Ravana himself, slain by Rama with divine assistance.

After Ravana's death, Sita undergoes the Agni Pariksha (trial by fire) to prove her purity. She emerges unscathed, affirming her chastity. The trio returns to Ayodhya, where Rama is crowned king, marking the end of their exile.

Teachings

- **Triumph of Good Over Evil**:

The battle between Rama and Ravana symbolizes the eternal conflict between good and evil. Ravana, despite his wisdom and strength, is ultimately defeated because of his pride and disregard for dharma. The war teaches that while evil may appear strong temporarily, righteousness will always prevail in the end. It emphasizes the need to stand firm for justice, no matter the odds.

- **Faith and Resilience**:

Sita's Agni Pariksha (trial by fire) after Ravana's defeat tests her purity. Sita's emergence unscathed affirms her steadfastness and purity. Her trial teaches that true inner strength is built on faith, patience, and resilience in the face of external doubts and challenges.

- **Unity in Diversity**:

The cooperation between humans and Vanaras, different species united for a common cause, emphasizes the importance of diversity in achieving goals. It teaches that unity, despite differences, is a powerful force that can overcome even the most formidable challenges.

7. Uttarakanda (The Final Section)

In this poignant Summary, Rama faces the painful task of exiling Sita due to doubts raised by his subjects about her chastity. Sita, now pregnant, takes refuge in Sage Valmiki's ashram, where she gives birth to Lava and Kusha.

Years later, Rama meets his sons during a yajna. Sita, unwilling to prove herself again, asks Mother Earth to take her back, and the earth swallows her. Rama, after fulfilling his earthly duties, returns to Vaikuntha as Lord Vishnu

Teachings

- **Leadership and Responsibility:**

Rama's decision to exile Sita, despite his personal feelings, underscores the idea that leadership often requires difficult decisions for the welfare of society. His action, though painful, shows that a ruler must prioritize the welfare of the kingdom over personal desires. It teaches that leadership involves making choices that benefit the collective, even at personal cost.

- **Inner Strength:**

Sita's refusal to undergo a second trial, and her ultimate return to Mother Earth, teaches that inner strength comes from self-acceptance and integrity. Sita's calm acceptance of her fate emphasizes the power of resilience and the importance of staying true to oneself in the face of injustice.

- **The Cycle of Life:**

Rama's eventual return to Vaikuntha symbolizes the cycle of life and death. The end of his earthly existence reminds us that everything in the material world is temporary, and the ultimate goal of life is spiritual liberation. This teaches that the soul is eternal, and one's duty is to live in accordance with dharma until the time comes to leave this world. The Ramayana offers timeless lessons on devotion, duty, and righteousness. Each Kanda presents profound teachings that guide individuals toward a virtuous life. Lord Rama's journey is not just a story of divine triumph but a spiritual roadmap for humanity, inspiring faith, courage, and commitment to dharma.

Chapter Two - The Raghu Dynasty

The **Raghu Vansh** (Dynasty of Raghu) is one of the most illustrious dynasties in Indian mythology, originating from the **Suryavansha (Solar Dynasty)**. It is named after King Raghu, known for his valor and righteousness. Below is a detailed hierarchy of the Raghu Vansh, as mentioned in various texts like Ramayana, Mahabharata, Harivamsha, and Raghuvamsa by Kalidasa.

1. Origin of Suryavansha

The Raghu Vansh traces its lineage to the Sun God (**Surya**).

- **Surya → Vaivasvata Manu** (the progenitor of mankind)

- Vaivasvata Manu's descendants led to the establishment of the Suryavansha, culminating in Ikshvaku.

2. Founding of the Raghu Vansh

- **Ikshvaku**: The first prominent king of the Suryavansha, son of Vaivasvata Manu. He established the kingdom of Ayodhya.

- Several successors ruled after Ikshvaku, maintaining the ideals of dharma and governance. Among them were:

o   **Kukshi**

o   **Vikukshi (Sasada)**

o   **Puranjaya (Indradhwaja)**: Known for his conquests and alliance with the gods.

o   **Mandhata**: A legendary ruler who expanded the dynasty's fame.

3. Notable Kings before Raghu

1.   **Yuvanasva**: A unique king who bore a son, Mandhata, after drinking sacred water.

2.   **Ambarisha**: A righteous king celebrated for his devotion to dharma and Lord Vishnu.

3.   **Satyavrata (Trishanku)**: Known for his aspiration to ascend to heaven in his mortal body.

4.   **Harishchandra**: A paragon of truth and sacrifice, celebrated in Indian mythology for his trials and adherence to truth.

4. King Raghu and the Raghu Vansh

•   **Raghu**: A mighty and virtuous king from whom the dynasty derives its name. Known for his valor, generosity, and adherence to dharma, Raghu expanded the glory of the dynasty through conquests and righteous rule.

5. Prominent Descendants of Raghu

1.   **Aja**: Raghu's son and the father of Dasharatha. He was known for his love and devotion to his wife, Indumati.

2.   **Dasharatha**: One of the most celebrated kings of the dynasty and father of Rama, Lakshmana, Bharata, and Shatrughna. His life was marked by tragedy due to his inadvertent curse by Shravan Kumar's parents.

3.   **Rama**: The central figure of the Ramayana, an incarnation of Vishnu, and the epitome of dharma. Rama's rule, referred to as Rama Rajya, became synonymous with justice, prosperity, and ideal governance.

4.   **Lakshmana, Bharata, and Shatrughna**: Rama's brothers, each of whom contributed significantly to the dynasty's legacy through their loyalty, sacrifices, and governance.

6. Subsequent Generations of the Raghu Vansh

After Rama, the dynasty continued through his sons and descendants:

1.   **Kusha and Lava**: Sons of Rama and Sita. They carried forward the lineage, with Kusha ruling Kushavati and Lava ruling Shravasti.

2.   **Atithi**: Kusha's son, who maintained the legacy of dharma.

3.   **Nishadha → Nala → Nabha → Pundarika**

4.   **Kshemadhanva → Devanika → Ahinagu**

5.   **Paripatra → Dala → Chhala → Uktha → Vajranabha**

6.   **Shankhana → Vyushitashva → Vishvasaha**

7.   **Brihadbala**: A descendant of Rama who fought and was killed in the Mahabharata war by Abhimanyu.

Illustrations

After Lord Rama, the glorious lineage of the Raghu Vansh continued through his sons and their descendants. This section details the rulers who upheld the legacy of dharma and governance, along with significant events in their reigns. Although not all their lives are extensively documented in the scriptures, the available references provide insights into their contributions.

A. Linage of Rama

1. Kusha and Lava

• **Kusha**: Rama's elder son with Sita, Kusha inherited his father's ideals and virtues. He was crowned the king of Kushavati, a city established by him. Kusha was known for his valor, wisdom, and adherence to dharma, much like his father. His reign marked the continuation of prosperity and justice in the kingdom.

o   **Marriage and Family**: Kusha married Kumudvati, a virtuous princess, and they had a son named Atithi, who succeeded him.

•   **Lava**: Rama's younger son, Lava, was given the kingdom of Shravasti to rule. Lava's reign also reflected the values instilled by his father. His sense of justice and governance ensured the flourishing of his kingdom. Lava's legacy is often celebrated alongside Kusha's for upholding the moral and ethical framework of the Raghu Vansh.

2. Atithi

•   **Atithi**: The son of Kusha, Atithi carried forward the lineage of the Raghu Vansh. Descriptions of his reign are sparse, but he is noted as a wise and just king who maintained the traditions of his forebears.

o   His name, meaning "guest," symbolizes hospitality and generosity, qualities attributed to his rule.

3. Nishadha to Pundarika

Following Atithi, the lineage included a series of rulers, each contributing to the dynasty in their way:

•   **Nishadha**: A righteous and able ruler known for his focus on governance and justice.

• **Nala**: Nishadha's son, who maintained the glory of the dynasty through his wisdom and leadership.

• **Nabha**: A king with a peaceful reign, Nabha upheld the traditions of truth and fairness in his kingdom.

• **Pundarika**: Known for his devotion to dharma and spiritual pursuits, he ensured a balance between material prosperity and spiritual well-being for his subjects.

4. Kshemadhanva to Ahinagu

The Raghu Vansh continued to flourish through the descendants of Pundarika:

• **Kshemadhanva**: An efficient king who safeguarded his kingdom from external threats and maintained internal harmony.

• **Devanika**: His reign was marked by advancements in governance and the arts.

• **Ahinagu**: A fearless king, Ahinagu is remembered for his contributions to the military strength of the dynasty and his dedication to justice.

5. Paripatra to Vajranabha

The lineage further expanded through successive kings:

- **Paripatra**: Known for his administrative skills and diplomatic acumen, he strengthened alliances with neighboring kingdoms.

- **Dala**: A king who was highly respected for his wisdom and fair judgment.

- **Chhala**: He upheld the dharma-centric governance that was the hallmark of the Raghu Vansh.

- **Uktha**: Known for his piety, Uktha focused on the spiritual development of his subjects.

- **Vajranabha**: A powerful king who restored the dynasty's military might and ensured its prosperity.

6. Shankhana to Vishvasaha

- **Shankhana**: A king with a vision for growth and development, he emphasized the importance of education and trade in his kingdom.

- **Vyushitashva**: Known for his compassion, Vyushitashva was loved by his subjects for his efforts to improve their lives.

- **Vishvasaha**: His reign marked the continuation of the dynasty's tradition of righteous rule.

7. Brihadbala

- **Brihadbala**: The last known prominent ruler of the Raghu Vansh. He appears in the Mahabharata as a warrior who fought on the side of the Kauravas in the Kurukshetra war.

o   **Significance in the War**: Brihadbala was slain by Abhimanyu, the valiant son of Arjuna, during the battle. His death marked the symbolic fading of the Raghu Vansh's glory in active politics and warfare.

Summary of Contributions

The subsequent generations of the Raghu Vansh may not have achieved the legendary status of Rama or Raghu, but their reigns collectively ensured the continuity of dharma-centric governance, prosperity, and the values that defined the dynasty. Each king, in his unique way, contributed to the lasting legacy of the Suryavansha and left an indelible mark on Indian history and mythology.

The lineage's eventual decline represents the cyclical nature of time (kala chakra) but also immortalizes their commitment to dharma, which remains an inspiration to this day.

The lineage of **Lakshmana**, **Bharata**, and **Shatrughna**, the three brothers of Lord Rama, continued through their descendants, forming sub-lineages within the Raghu Vansh. Each of them played pivotal roles during their lives and left behind a legacy of dharma and valor. Here is a detailed account of their lineages as recorded in various scriptures:

B. Lineage of Lakshmana

Lakshmana, the most loyal brother of Rama, was deeply devoted to his elder brother. After Lord Rama's reign, Lakshmana's legacy continued through his sons.

Sons of Lakshmana

• **Angada**: The elder son of Lakshmana. Named after the loyal Vanara warrior Angada from the Ramayana, he was known for his bravery and leadership qualities.

• **Chandraketu**: The younger son, who inherited his father's virtues of loyalty and righteousness.

Legacy of Angada and Chandraketu

• Angada was given the kingdom of **Karakata**, a territory separate from Ayodhya, by Lord Rama after his return from exile. His rule was marked by wisdom, valor, and adherence to dharma.

• Chandraketu ruled the kingdom of **Madhupuri**, a prosperous region. He established a legacy of just and righteous governance, continuing the ideals of the Raghu Vansh.

C. Lineage of Bharata

Bharata, the epitome of sacrifice and devotion, ruled Ayodhya during Rama's exile and later governed his own region after Lord Rama's coronation. His sons carried forward his legacy.

Sons of Bharata

- **Taksha**: The elder son, who became the ruler of **Takshashila** (modern Taxila, in present-day Pakistan).

- **Pushkala**: The younger son, who established and ruled the city of **Pushkalavati** (modern Charsadda, in Pakistan).

Legacy of Taksha and Pushkala

- Taksha is remembered for his military prowess and administrative skills. He expanded his kingdom and upheld the dharma-centric governance of the Raghu Vansh.

- Pushkala ruled Pushkalavati with fairness and prosperity. Both cities became centers of culture and learning under their rule, preserving the glory of their lineage.

D. Lineage of Shatrughna

Shatrughna, the youngest brother of Rama, was known for his quiet strength, deep loyalty, and dedication to his family. After assisting his brothers in their respective endeavors, he carved out his own legacy.

Sons of Shatrughna

- **Subahu**: The elder son, who inherited his father's virtues of devotion and righteousness.

- **Shrutasena (or Shatrughati)**: The younger son, known for his courage and wisdom.

Legacy of Subahu and Shrutasena

• Subahu was crowned as the king of **Mathura**, which had been conquered by Shatrughna after defeating the demon Lavanasura. Under his rule, Mathura flourished as a prosperous kingdom.

• Shrutasena became a ruler of another territory, continuing the lineage of Shatrughna with justice and valor.

These sub-lineages expanded the influence of the Raghu Vansh, spreading its ideals of dharma and just governance far and wide. The sons of Lakshmana, Bharata, and Shatrughna contributed to maintaining the glory of their family while establishing their own independent legacies.

Chapter Three - Is it possible to connect Ramayana and Mahabharata?

The connections between the **Ramayana** and **Mahabharata** periods are subtle but significant, linking the legendary **Raghu Vansh** of the Ramayana to the events of the Mahabharata. These connections primarily highlight the dynastic continuity and the interplay of dharma across the two epic narratives. Let us explore these links in detail, beginning with **Brihadbala**, the last prominent ruler of the Raghu Vansh.

Legacy of Raghu Vansh

The Raghu Vansh epitomized the ideals of dharma, valor, and justice. Kings of this dynasty were revered for their adherence to truth and their contributions to the welfare of their subjects. The lineage faded over time but remains immortalized in epics and scriptures as the epitome of royal excellence.

This hierarchy reflects the grandeur of the dynasty, whose influence extended beyond the Ramayana and into the broader framework of Indian mythology and history.

1. Brihadbala; A Key Connection

Brihadbala, a descendant of Lord Rama, serves as a direct connection between the Ramayana and Mahabharata periods.

- **Lineage**: Brihadbala belonged to the illustrious **Ikshvaku dynasty** and was a king of the **Kosala Kingdom**. His ancestor Kusha, Lord Rama's son, continued the Raghu Vansh, and generations later, Brihadbala emerged as one of its rulers.

- **Role in the Mahabharata**: Brihadbala fought on the side of the **Kauravas** during the Kurukshetra War. He was slain by **Abhimanyu**, the young and valiant son of Arjuna, during the **Chakravyuha battle**.

o This tragic end symbolizes the fading influence of the once-glorious Raghu Vansh and highlights the cyclical nature of dharma and adharma across epochs.

2. Lineage Overlap and Dynastic Continuity

Both epics trace their protagonists to the **Solar Dynasty (Suryavansha)** and **Lunar Dynasty (Chandravansha)**, with the Raghu Vansh forming a branch of the Suryavansha. The dynastic interconnections bridge the two periods:

- The Ikshvaku dynasty, to which Lord Rama belonged, represents the Ramayana's Suryavansha lineage.

- The Lunar Dynasty, to which the Pandavas and Kauravas belonged, is prominent in the Mahabharata.

- Through time, the descendants of these dynasties interacted, with the fading prominence of the Suryavansha seen in Brihadbala's participation in the Mahabharata.

3. Presence of Ancient Structures and Traditions

Several places and traditions from the Ramayana era are referenced in the Mahabharata:

• **Ayodhya**: The Kosala Kingdom remained prominent during the Mahabharata period, with Ayodhya still recognized as a significant city. Brihadbala ruled this region, showing the continuity of the Ikshvaku lineage.

• **Janaka's Lineage**: The teachings and legacy of King Janaka, Sita's father, had lasting philosophical influence, particularly in spiritual traditions. His association with **Brahma Vidya** is referenced in the Mahabharata as a guiding principle for dharma.

• **Mithila and Videha**: Regions associated with Sita's lineage remained culturally influential during the Mahabharata period.

4. Rishi Connections

The sages and rishis who played crucial roles in the Ramayana period continued to influence the Mahabharata epoch:

• **Vashishtha**: The royal guru of the Ikshvaku dynasty in the Ramayana was a key figure in transmitting dharmic values, and his lineage of disciples impacted the Mahabharata.

• **Vishvamitra**: Another key sage in the Ramayana, his spiritual contributions and teachings influenced later generations.

•   **Durvasa**: Known for his temper and boons, Durvasa appears in both epics. In the Mahabharata, he is connected with Kunti, granting her the boon to invoke divine beings.

•   **Narada**: The celestial sage is a linking figure, appearing in both epics to guide, warn, or advise key characters.

5. Philosophical and Ethical Parallels

Both the Ramayana and Mahabharata explore the nature of dharma, albeit in different contexts:

•   **Ramayana**: Dharma is portrayed as an absolute ideal, exemplified by Rama's adherence to duty, truth, and sacrifice.

•   **Mahabharata**: Dharma is shown in a more complex light, with shades of gray as characters like Yudhishthira and Krishna navigate difficult moral dilemmas.

•   The continuity of dharma as a guiding principle connects the two epics, with the Mahabharata often referencing the ideals established during the Ramayana.

6. Shared Themes and Characters

Several characters and themes overlap between the two epics:

•   **Hanuman**: Hanuman, a central figure in the Ramayana, appears briefly in the Mahabharata. Bhima, a Pandava, meets Hanuman during his search for the Saugandhika flower. Hanuman blesses Bhima, affirming the connection between the two eras.

•   **The Concept of Exile**: The themes of exile and return (Rama's exile, the Pandavas' exile) show the continuity of trials faced by dharmic rulers.

•   **Divine Interventions**: Vishnu's incarnations (Rama and Krishna) underscore the recurring divine effort to restore cosmic balance.

The Ramayana and Mahabharata are deeply interwoven through shared dynasties, characters, and philosophies. Brihadbala's participation in the Mahabharata serves as a symbolic link between these two epic eras, demonstrating the cyclical progression of dharma across generations. The legacy of the Raghu Vansh, while fading in military dominance by the Mahabharata period, continues to shine through its enduring ideals and contributions to Indian history and culture.

Chapter Four - Insignificant Characters who contributed significantly

1. Jatayu

Jatayu, the noble vulture, was a close friend of Dasharatha and a symbol of courage and loyalty. Despite his old age, Jatayu displayed unmatched valor when he confronted Ravana as the demon king abducted Sita. He fought fiercely, trying to stop Ravana's chariot mid-air, only to be mortally wounded. Before his death, Jatayu provided crucial information to Rama and Lakshmana about the direction Ravana took Sita. His sacrifice highlighted the theme of selfless devotion to dharma. Jatayu's actions made him a pivotal character in the epic, emphasizing that one's worth is defined by deeds, not status or strength.

Jatayu, the noble vulture king, was a symbol of courage and loyalty. Despite his age and frailty, he selflessly attempted to rescue Sita when Ravana abducted her. His strength lay in his unwavering devotion to dharma and his commitment to justice. Jatayu fought valiantly against Ravana, showcasing his physical and moral might, even though he was gravely outmatched. His act of bravery cost him his life, but it altered the course of the epic by providing Rama with crucial information about Sita's abduction. His sacrifice was a pivotal moment that set Rama firmly on the path to Lanka, ensuring Ravana's downfall.

2. Guha

Guha, the Nishada chief, was a tribal king and a loyal friend of Rama. When Rama, Sita, and Lakshmana embarked on their 14-year exile, Guha warmly welcomed them to his territory, offering them hospitality and unwavering support. He even provided them a safe passage across the Ganga River, demonstrating his devotion to dharma. Guha's respect for Rama transcended social boundaries, showcasing harmony among diverse communities. Though his role in the story is brief; his selflessness and loyalty left a lasting impression, reminding readers of the importance of friendships and alliances in overcoming challenges.

Guha, the king of the Nishadas, exemplified selfless friendship and loyalty. His devotion to Rama was unwavering as he welcomed the exiled prince with open arms. Guha provided shelter and resources, enabling Rama, Sita, and Lakshmana to cross the Ganga and begin their journey into the forest. His strength lay in his simplicity and his dedication to dharma, showing no hesitation in helping Rama despite his humble background. Guha's actions highlighted the unity among diverse communities in aiding Rama's mission, reinforcing the idea that greatness transcends caste or status.

3. Shabari's Guru (Matanga Rishi)

Matanga Rishi, though not directly visible in most retellings, played a significant role in shaping Shabari's devotion to Rama. He mentored her on the path of spirituality and instructed her to wait for the arrival of Rama, recognizing him as an incarnation of Vishnu. Through his wisdom, Matanga ensured that Shabari's life became a beacon of devotion and service. His teachings indirectly influenced Rama's journey, as Shabari guided him toward Sugriva and the Vanaras. Matanga represents the unseen mentors in our lives, whose wisdom may not always be evident but who leave profound impacts on destiny.

Matanga Rishi was a saint known for his spiritual wisdom and foresight. He instructed Shabari to wait for Rama, assuring her that her devotion would bear fruit. His teachings emphasized devotion and humility, inspiring Shabari to lead a life of selflessness. Matanga Rishi's guidance indirectly led to Rama meeting Shabari, who directed him to Sugriva and Hanuman. This encounter was instrumental in forming alliances that eventually led to the victory over Ravana.

4. Angada

The son of Vali and Tara, Angada initially harbored resentment toward Sugriva for his father's death. However, he grew into a loyal ally of Rama during the battle against Ravana. His mission as an envoy to Ravana showcased his courage and diplomatic skill, as he boldly appealed to Ravana to surrender Sita and avoid war. Angada's unwavering dedication to Rama and his ability to motivate the Vanara army added strength to their cause. His role underscores the potential for growth and redemption, demonstrating that even those burdened by loss can rise to become key contributors to a greater purpose.

Angada, the son of Vali, displayed immense strength, loyalty, and resilience. Despite his father's tragic death, Angada chose to serve Rama selflessly. His diplomatic skills and courage were evident when he approached Ravana's court as Rama's emissary, urging Ravana to surrender Sita. Angada's actions demonstrated his devotion to dharma and the greater good. His role in the war, especially in leading the Vanara troops, significantly contributed to the success of Rama's mission.

Angada's mission to Ravana's court, often referred to as **Angada Shishtayee**, is one of the most dramatic moments in the Ramayana. It is not merely an episode of challenge but also a powerful moral discourse delivered in the midst of a hostile audience. Angada's words and actions highlight his intellect, strength, and unwavering loyalty to Rama. Below is a detailed account of the event, including his dialogues and actions:

Angada's Arrival in Ravana's Court

Rama sends Angada as an emissary to Ravana with a final diplomatic message, urging him to return Sita and avoid bloodshed. Angada, a young warrior of unmatched valor and Vali's son, enters Ravana's magnificent court fearlessly, despite the presence of powerful Rakshasas like Indrajit, Kumbhakarna (not yet awakened), and other demon generals. His demeanor is calm but commanding, exuding the confidence of someone on the side of dharma.

Dialogue with Ravana

Standing tall, Angada addresses Ravana with respect but firmness:

• "Mighty Ravana, I come here not to praise you but to warn you. You are known as a great king, a scholar, and a warrior. Yet, blinded by arrogance, you have committed an unforgivable sin by abducting Sita, the chaste wife of Lord Rama. Return her, and peace will prevail. Continue on this path of adharma, and your kingdom will face annihilation."

Ravana, seated arrogantly on his throne, laughs mockingly, dismissing Angada's warnings:

• "Who are you to speak of annihilation to me, Ravana, conqueror of the three worlds? Go back to your prince and tell him that his days are numbered. My strength and my army are invincible."

Angada retorts sharply, his words laced with wisdom and challenge:

•   "Your invincibility is an illusion, Ravana. You have gained your power through boons, but you misuse it against dharma. The forces of righteousness may seem small to you, but their strength lies in truth. Lord Rama's army of Vanaras will defeat your legions, for dharma always triumphs over adharma."

The Foot Challenge: Angada's Act of Defiance

Ravana, enraged by Angada's words, orders his ministers and warriors to capture him. Unfazed, Angada plants his foot firmly on the ground and declares:

•   "If anyone among you is capable of moving my foot, I shall willingly surrender and take your orders. But if you fail, it will prove that Rama's strength, not yours, is supreme."

One by one, Ravana's mightiest warriors, including Prahasta and Atikaya, try to lift or displace Angada's foot. Despite their enormous strength, none of them can budge it even slightly. Angada's strength, bolstered by his righteousness and devotion to Rama, remains immovable.

Confronting Ravana

Angada then turns directly to Ravana and, in a voice filled with authority, says:

•   "You boast of your power, Ravana, yet even your greatest warriors cannot move the foot of Rama's servant. How do you hope to stand against Rama himself? Return Sita now, or your pride will lead to your downfall. Your kingdom will burn, and your name will be cursed in history."

At this point, Ravana, filled with rage but also uneasy at Angada's confidence, rises from his throne. He considers attempting to displace Angada's foot himself but stops, sensing the moral weight of the challenge. Instead, he lashes out verbally:

•   "You speak boldly for a mere monkey. Leave now, or you will join the ranks of the dead before the battle even begins."

Angada's Exit

Angada, smiling defiantly, replies:

•   "You speak of death, Ravana, but it is you who stands on the brink of destruction. Rama has offered you peace, but your arrogance blinds you. Remember my words when Lanka burns and your empire falls."

With these words, Angada leaps out of the court and returns to Rama's camp, his mission of diplomacy complete.

Significance of the Episode

1.   Moral Victory: Angada's unshakable foot becomes a symbol of Rama's righteousness and the moral superiority of dharma over adharma.

2.   Foreshadowing Ravana's Downfall: Ravana's inability to accept Angada's warnings highlights his arrogance and sets the stage for his eventual defeat.

3.   Angada's Growth: This episode showcases Angada's maturity, intelligence, and loyalty, elevating him from a grieving prince to a key warrior in Rama's army.

4.   Message of Dharma: The incident underscores the timeless truth that physical might is futile without moral strength.

In Ravana's court, Angada does not merely represent Rama but embodies the virtues of humility, righteousness, and courage, leaving an indelible mark on the Ramayana.

5. Sugriva

Sugriva, the dethroned Vanara king, formed a crucial alliance with Rama, providing him access to a powerful army. Initially living in fear of Vali, Sugriva's transformation into a confident and capable leader after Vali's death marked his character arc. His loyalty to Rama and his coordination of the bridge-building and war efforts made him an indispensable ally. Sugriva's story also reflects themes of second chances and the importance of forming strategic partnerships. Despite his initial flaws, including a brief period of indulgence after reclaiming his throne, Sugriva ultimately fulfilled his promises to Rama with diligence.

Sugriva, the exiled king of Kishkindha, played a vital role in Rama's quest to rescue Sita. Initially hesitant, Sugriva forged an alliance with Rama after being assured of help in reclaiming his kingdom from Vali. Sugriva's strength lay in his strategic acumen, as he mobilized the Vanara army to search for Sita and fight against Ravana. His devotion to Rama and his selflessness in fulfilling his promises ensured the success of the mission, showcasing the importance of alliances and trust.

6. Sampati

Sampati, Jatayu's elder brother, played a pivotal role in revealing Sita's location to the Vanaras. Aged and grounded due to his damaged wings, Sampati had witnessed Ravana taking Sita to Lanka. His revelation reinvigorated the Vanara search party, giving them the direction they desperately needed. Sampati's back-story of losing his wings while saving Jatayu from the sun further added depth to his character, highlighting his sacrificial nature. His role demonstrates how even those who appear powerless can contribute significantly to a noble cause when guided by purpose and wisdom.

Sampati displayed remarkable wisdom and devotion when he revealed Sita's location to Rama's allies. Despite being physically weakened, his information became a turning point in the search for Sita. Sampati's actions highlighted the value of knowledge and timely intervention. His devotion to his brother and his selflessness in aiding Rama's mission emphasized the interconnectedness of characters in achieving a greater purpose.

7. Mandodari's Father (Mayasura)

Mayasura, the demon architect, was a significant yet understated figure in the Ramayana. As Mandodari's father, he provided Ravana with not only his brilliant daughter but also architectural marvels such as the Pushpaka Vimana and Lanka's grand palace. These creations underscored the opulence of Ravana's kingdom and provided the setting for many key events in the epic. Mayasura's craftsmanship symbolizes the importance of art and innovation in shaping history. Despite his allegiance to asuras, his legacy as an unparalleled creator transcended moral binaries, adding layers to the epic's narrative.

Mayasura, a renowned architect and asura king, symbolized resourcefulness and foresight. Though not a central figure in the Ramayana; his creation of the Lanka palace and Pushpaka Vimana indirectly influenced the course of events. Mayasura's legacy as a master craftsman demonstrated the importance of skill and ingenuity. His gifts became tools of power and wealth for Ravana, but their misuse ultimately led to Lanka's downfall, underscoring the consequences of dharma violation.

8. Kumbhakarna

Kumbhakarna, Ravana's gigantic brother, is remembered for his towering presence and complex character. A formidable warrior with immense strength, Kumbhakarna was loyal to Ravana despite disagreeing with his unethical decisions. His tragic flaw was his inability to break free from his familial obligations, leading to his eventual death in battle. Kumbhakarna's reluctance to fight and his acknowledgment of Rama's righteousness portray him as a tragic hero. His story underscores the internal conflict between dharma and loyalty, adding emotional depth to the epic's exploration of human virtues and failings.

Kumbhakarna, Ravana's giant brother, was a paradoxical character embodying immense strength and deep wisdom. Despite his loyalty to Ravana, Kumbhakarna recognized his brother's flaws and advised him to return Sita. Bound by his sense of duty, he fought against Rama's forces, displaying unmatched bravery and devotion to family. His death symbolized the destruction of misguided loyalty and served as a reminder of the consequences of siding with adharma.

9. Lava and Kusha

Rama's twin sons, Lava and Kusha, played a vital role in perpetuating the Ramayana. Raised by Sita under Valmiki's care, the twins grew into skilled warriors and scholars. They unknowingly confronted their father during a conflict, showcasing their valor and righteousness. Their recital of the Ramayana brought Rama's story to the people, ensuring its immortality. Lava and Kusha's innocence, combined with their strength and wisdom, symbolized the continuity of dharma across generations. Their role also reconciled the narrative's tragic elements by bringing Sita and Rama's legacy full circle.

Lava and Kusha the twin sons of Rama and Sita epitomized innocence, strength, and devotion to dharma. Raised by Sita in sage Valmiki's ashram, they grew into skilled warriors and scholars. Their confrontation with Rama during the Ashvamedha Yajna revealed their valor and adherence to dharma. Their actions reunited the estranged family and brought closure to Sita's story, symbolizing the continuity of dharma through future generations.

10. Malyavan

Malyavan, an elder statesman in Ravana's court, served as the voice of reason. His advice to Ravana to return Sita and avoid war highlighted his wisdom and deep understanding of dharma. Although his counsel was ignored, Malyavan's character symbolizes the recurring theme of unheeded wisdom in the Ramayana. His role reminds readers of the tragic consequences of arrogance and the importance of listening to sage advice. Malyavan's presence added a layer of complexity to Ravana's court, illustrating the existence of differing perspectives even within a villain's circle. Being a wise counselor in Ravana's court, he urged Ravana repeatedly to return Sita showcasing his strength of character and devotion to the greater good. Malyavan's foresight highlighted the importance of wise advisors and the tragic consequences of ignoring dharma. His presence emphasized the need for ethical leadership in governance.

Chapter Five - Influence of prominent Female Characters

1. Shabari

Shabari was a tribal woman of unmatched devotion to Rama. Living in a hermitage under the guidance of Matanga Rishi, she awaited Rama for years, as her guru prophesied his arrival. Shabari's simplicity and love were evident when she offered Rama berries, tasting each to ensure their sweetness a gesture that showed her devotion transcended societal norms. Rama not only accepted her offerings but also blessed her, emphasizing the equality of all devotees, regardless of caste or background. Shabari's role highlights the purity of devotion and how small acts of faith can resonate profoundly in the epic's larger narrative.

Shabari's defection from her tribal community

Shabari's defection from her tribal community is a powerful narrative of faith, devotion, and spiritual transcendence. Her decision to leave behind her traditional life and dedicate herself to the path of *dharma* and her guru's teachings is a testament to her unwavering determination and devotion to righteousness.

Shabari's Background

Shabari belonged to a tribal community that lived a simple, nature-bound life. These communities were often excluded from mainstream society and were considered untouchable by many in the Vedic culture of the time. Despite her humble background, Shabari exhibited a strong moral compass and spiritual yearning from an early age. She was deeply compassionate and sought meaning beyond the customs and rituals of her tribe.

The Turning Point: Encounter with Sage Matanga

Shabari's defection began when she encountered Sage Matanga, a revered rishi who lived near the forests of Rishyamukha.

- **Role of Matanga**: Shabari observed the sage's spiritual practices and teachings, which focused on *dharma* (righteousness), universal love, and devotion to the divine.

- **Moment of Awakening**: Inspired by his wisdom, she realized that her tribal community's way of life—though rooted in nature—did not align with the higher spiritual truths she sought. This inner awakening set the stage for her eventual separation from her community.

The Act of Defection

Shabari's defection wasn't an act of rebellion or disrespect but a quiet and resolute choice to walk the path of spirituality.

• **Conflict with Tribal Customs**: Her community adhered to strict tribal customs and rituals, which often revolved around their traditional beliefs. They viewed her association with a Vedic sage as an act of betrayal.

• **Breaking Social Norms**: By choosing to serve Sage Matanga and dedicate herself to spiritual practices, Shabari broke away from the societal expectations and norms of her community. This was a significant departure, as it involved leaving behind her family, friends, and way of life.

The Price of Defection

• **Alienation**: Shabari's decision was met with disapproval and rejection by her community. Many viewed her as a defector who had abandoned her people's customs.

• **Isolation**: After Sage Matanga's death, Shabari lived alone in the forest. However, this solitude did not deter her; instead, it deepened her connection to the divine.

The Life of Devotion

Shabari's defection was not a retreat from the world but a step toward a higher purpose. She dedicated her life to serving her guru's memory and awaiting Lord Rama, as Matanga had prophesied that Rama would visit her one day.

• **Simplicity and Faith**: Shabari's life was marked by simplicity. She lived in a humble hut, subsisted on forest fruits, and spent her days in meditation and devotion.

• **Service to Rama**: When Rama and Lakshmana visited her, she offered them fruits that she had carefully tasted to ensure they were sweet—a gesture of pure love and devotion. Her humility and faith moved Rama, who blessed her with liberation (*moksha*).

Symbolism of Shabari's Defection

Shabari's defection represents a transcendence of societal boundaries and prejudices:

• **Breaking Social Barriers**: By associating with a tribal woman, Rama demonstrated that *dharma* and devotion are not limited by caste, creed, or social status.

• **Faith Over Rituals**: Shabari's life emphasized that true spirituality lies in faith, devotion, and love, not in rituals or societal expectations.

• **Women in Spirituality**: Shabari's story also highlights women's role in spiritual discourse, showing that devotion and righteousness are accessible to all, regardless of gender or background.

Lessons from Shabari's Defection

1.   **Courage to Follow the Truth**: Shabari's decision to leave her community reflects the courage to follow her inner truth, even when it meant facing rejection.

2.   **Faith in Prophecy**: Her unwavering belief in her guru's words and her patient wait for Rama underline the power of faith and devotion.

3.   **Universal Dharma**: Shabari's story exemplifies the universality of *dharma*, transcending social hierarchies and customs.

Shabari's defection from her tribal community was not just a departure from tradition but a transformative journey toward spiritual enlightenment. It stands as a timeless example of how faith and devotion can elevate individuals above societal limitations.

2. Mandodari

Mandodari, Ravana's wife, was a wise and virtuous queen. Despite being married to one of the most powerful asuras, she upheld dharma and constantly advised Ravana to release Sita and avoid unnecessary conflict. Her foresight and moral compass made her a voice of reason in the otherwise turbulent Lanka. Mandodari's anguish after Ravana's death humanized the epic's villain, showing the emotional toll of his actions on his loved ones. She symbolizes the strength and resilience of women caught in the crossfire of male ambition, often bearing the consequences of choices they do not support.

Mandodari, the queen consort of Ravana in the Ramayana, is portrayed as a figure of immense grace, intelligence, and moral strength. Her life, particularly before and after Sita's abduction, reflects the dynamics of her character as a loyal wife, a wise advisor, and a symbol of virtue amidst chaos.

Mandodari's Life before Sita's Abduction

Mandodari, born to Mayasura (a demon architect) and Hema (a celestial nymph), was a figure of exceptional beauty and wisdom. As a princess of the Danavas, she grew up surrounded by knowledge, art, and the mysteries of divine architecture. Despite her asura lineage, Mandodari was known for her righteous conduct and devotion to dharma.

When she married Ravana, the king of Lanka, she became a key figure in the court, admired for her poise and intellect. Ravana, a formidable king and a scholar, respected Mandodari's wisdom, often seeking her counsel on matters of statecraft. Though she loved Ravana deeply, she was not blind to his flaws, particularly his arrogance and unchecked ambition. Mandodari played a crucial role in maintaining the balance in the royal household, serving as a calming influence on Ravana and his siblings.

Her life in Lanka before Sita's abduction was one of relative peace and prosperity. The kingdom flourished under Ravana's rule, with Mandodari presiding over a court that admired her as much for her beauty as for her sagacity. However, as Ravana's thirst for power grew, she began to sense the shadows of impending doom. Her frequent attempts to counsel him against unethical actions, like his treatment of women and overreaching ambitions, often went unheeded.

Life after Sita's Abduction

The abduction of Sita marked a turning point in Mandodari's life. When Ravana brought Sita to Lanka, Mandodari was dismayed by his actions. She immediately recognized the moral and strategic folly of abducting the wife of Rama, a prince of great virtue and valor. Mandodari warned Ravana of the dire consequences of his actions, urging him to return Sita to avoid a disastrous war. However, Ravana, blinded by his obsession and arrogance, dismissed her advice.

As the war drew closer, Mandodari's life became a tumult of fear and helplessness. She witnessed Ravana's stubbornness lead him to alienate his closest allies, including Bibhishan, his own brother, who defected to Rama's side. Mandodari's attempts to mediate between Ravana and those who opposed his decisions showcased her resilience and her commitment to protecting her family and kingdom.

- During the war, Mandodari endured immense personal grief. She mourned the loss of her sons, Akshaya Kumar and Indrajit (Meghnad), who were killed in the battle. Despite her sorrow, she maintained her dignity, standing by Ravana even as his empire crumbled around them. Her unwavering loyalty was not born of ignorance but of her deep love and sense of duty toward her husband and kingdom.

After Ravana's Death

Following Ravana's defeat and death at the hands of Rama, Mandodari's sorrow was profound. She lamented not only the loss of her husband but also the downfall of Lanka, which she had so diligently tried to prevent. In her poignant lamentation over Ravana's body, she acknowledged his greatness as a king and scholar but also expressed her sorrow for his failure to heed the voice of reason and dharma.

After the war, Mandodari's life took on a quieter, reflective tone. She played a key role in ensuring that the transition of power in Lanka was smooth, supporting Bibhishan, Ravana's righteous brother, as the new king. Despite her grief, Mandodari's wisdom and resilience made her a source of inspiration for the people of Lanka during their time of recovery.

Mandodari's life, especially after Sita's abduction, highlights the tragedy of a queen bound by love and duty to a flawed king. Her story is a poignant reminder of the strength of character and the enduring power of righteousness, even in the face of overwhelming adversity.

3. Ahalya

Ahalya, the wife of Sage Gautama, represents redemption and forgiveness in the Ramayana. Cursed to become a stone for her transgression; whether intentional or a result of deception: her story gained prominence when Rama liberated her from the curse with his touch. A detailed characterization of Ahalya is given in Chapter sixteen.

4. Kaikeyi's Maid Manthara

Manthara, Kaikeyi's manipulative maid, played a critical yet overlooked role in the epic. Her instigation prompted Kaikeyi to demand Rama's exile and Bharata's coronation. Despite her negative portrayal, Manthara's actions were pivotal in setting the narrative in motion, leading to Rama's exile, the abduction of Sita, and the eventual destruction of Ravana. Manthara's cunning nature symbolizes the ripple effects of greed and jealousy, serving as a cautionary tale about the power of influence and the consequences of short-sighted desires.

Manthara, the nursemaid and confidante of Queen Kaikeyi in the Ramayana, is often depicted as the catalyst for the events that lead to Rama's exile.

However, a deeper exploration of her life and motivations reveals a more complex character than the traditionally villainous image often portrayed. Manthara's actions, while misguided, stem from a combination of loyalty, fear, and personal history.

Manthara's Early Life

Manthara's origins are not widely elaborated upon in most versions of the Ramayana, but it is evident that she was a servant of considerable intelligence and cunning. Born into a humble background, Manthara rose to prominence in the royal household due to her unwavering loyalty to Kaikeyi. She was a keen observer, deeply familiar with the nuances of palace politics, and devoted her life to serving Kaikeyi from the queen's childhood.

As Kaikeyi's nursemaid, Manthara was more than a servant; she was a maternal figure, confidante, and advisor. Her closeness to Kaikeyi was born of genuine care, and she often prioritized the queen's interests above all else. Her loyalty was fierce, but it was also tinged with possessiveness, making her wary of anyone or anything that might diminish Kaikeyi's stature or happiness.

Life in Ayodhya

In Ayodhya, Manthara's position as Kaikeyi's confidante allowed her to witness the inner workings of the court. She admired Kaikeyi's beauty, intelligence, and strength, and took pride in her role as a guiding figure. However, she was also acutely aware of the societal dynamics in the royal household. Despite Dasharatha's professed love for Kaikeyi, Manthara perceived subtle favoritism toward Kaushalya, Rama's mother, particularly in matters of succession and courtly respect.

Manthara's protective instincts for Kaikeyi were heightened by her awareness of Kaikeyi's precarious position. Though Kaikeyi was Dasharatha's favorite, Manthara feared that Kaushalya, as the senior queen, held greater influence. This fear was exacerbated by the impending coronation of Rama, which Manthara saw as a potential threat to Kaikeyi's status and the future of Bharata, Kaikeyi's son.

The Catalyst for Her Actions

Manthara's decision to instigate Kaikeyi to demand the boons promised by Dasharatha was not born out of malice but a combination of factors:

1.   Loyalty to Kaikeyi and Bharata: Manthara genuinely believed she was acting in Kaikeyi's and Bharata's best interests. She feared that Rama's ascension to the throne would marginalize Bharata and diminish Kaikeyi's influence in the court. Her protective nature drove her to take drastic measures to secure what she thought was Kaikeyi's rightful position as the mother of the future king.

2.   Fear of Marginalization: Having lived in the palace and observed the dynamics of royal succession, Manthara may have been influenced by stories of queens and princes sidelined after losing favor. She likely feared a similar fate for Kaikeyi and Bharata, especially if Kaushalya's son became king.

3.   Personal Insecurities: Manthara's own position in the palace hierarchy was tenuous. As a servant, she depended on Kaikeyi's favor for her survival and status. Any threat to Kaikeyi's standing was also a threat to Manthara's security.

4.   A Misguided Sense of Strategy: Manthara's intellect and understanding of palace politics were real, but her judgment was flawed. She underestimated the consequences of her plan, focusing solely on short-term gains for Kaikeyi and Bharata without considering the broader implications for the royal family and Ayodhya.

Manthara's Role in Convincing Kaikeyi

Manthara's manipulation of Kaikeyi was a masterclass in persuasion, born from years of understanding Kaikeyi's psychology. She appealed to Kaikeyi's pride, fear, and maternal instincts. By portraying Rama's coronation as a conspiracy to undermine Bharata, Manthara sowed seeds of doubt in Kaikeyi's mind. Her arguments were emotionally charged, emphasizing Kaikeyi's supposed neglect and the potential sidelining of Bharata.

Manthara's success in convincing Kaikeyi also highlights vulnerability in Kaikeyi's character: her deep love for Bharata, coupled with her fear of losing her position as Dasharatha's favorite queen. Kaikeyi, though wise and strong, was momentarily swayed by Manthara's impassioned arguments, leading her to demand Rama's exile and Bharata's coronation.

Life after the Exile Incident

Manthara's life after the exile of Rama was marked by regret and ostracization. While her actions succeeded in securing the boons for Kaikeyi, they backfired disastrously. Dasharatha's death, Kaikeyi's isolation from the royal family, and Bharata's refusal to accept the throne all served as bitter reminders of the fallout from her schemes. Manthara likely faced condemnation from the palace staff and the citizens of Ayodhya, who held her responsible for the tragedy.

Despite this, it is important to note that Manthara was not inherently evil. Her actions, though misguided, were driven by her love for Kaikeyi and her desire to protect her. In many ways, Manthara is a tragic figure; a woman whose loyalty and concern for her queen led her to make decisions that brought sorrow to all involved, including herself.

A Reinterpretation of Manthara's Legacy

Manthara's story is a reminder that even the most seemingly villainous characters have motivations rooted in their circumstances, fears, and loyalties. Her actions, while triggering a series of catastrophic events, also set the stage for Rama's exile, which ultimately led to his spiritual journey and the triumph of dharma.

In a more compassionate light, Manthara can be seen as a symbol of the unintended consequences of misguided loyalty and fear. Her life serves as a cautionary tale about the importance of wisdom and restraint, even in the face of perceived threats.

5. Tara

Tara, the wife of Vali, was a wise and strong Vanara queen. After Vali's death at the hands of Rama, she acted as a stabilizing force, calming her son Angada and preventing further discord. Tara's role as an advisor to Vali and later as a counselor to Sugriva emphasized her intellect and leadership qualities. Her pragmatic approach to conflict resolution made her a key figure in the Vanara kingdom's stability. Tara's character illustrates the often-overlooked political and emotional contributions of women in maintaining harmony during turbulent times.

6. Anasuya

Anasuya, the wife of Sage Atri, played a small but significant role in the Ramayana. When Rama and Sita visited her hermitage during their exile, Anasuya warmly received them and offered invaluable advice to

Sita on the duties of a devoted wife. She also gifted Sita divine garments and jewelry that helped her endure the hardships of forest life. Anasuya's wisdom and hospitality reflected the nurturing role of sages' wives in preserving dharma and guiding the protagonists.

Anusuya is one of the most celebrated women in Indian mythology, renowned for her unparalleled chastity, devotion, and virtuous nature. Her story exemplifies unwavering loyalty, selflessness, and spiritual power, making her a symbol of the ideal woman in Indian traditions. Below is a detailed narrative about her life and significance:

Lineage and Early Life

Anusuya was born to sage Kardama and his wife Devahuti, known for their immense piety and dedication to spiritual practices. From an early age, Anusuya exhibited extraordinary qualities of compassion, humility, and wisdom. Her name itself, derived from the Sanskrit root "Anasuya," means "free from envy or jealousy," reflecting her pure and virtuous character.

Marriage to Sage Atri

Anusuya married sage Atri, one of the Saptarishis (seven great sages) and a devout follower of Lord Brahma. Their union was based on mutual respect, spiritual alignment, and a shared commitment to the welfare of humanity. Together, they performed numerous penances and rituals to uphold dharma and promote spiritual knowledge among people.

Anusuya's Devotion and Chastity

Anusuya's chastity and devotion to her husband are legendary. Her unwavering adherence to the principles of dharma and her selfless nature earned her divine recognition. She is often regarded as a role model for married women, symbolizing the virtues of fidelity, humility, and service.

One of the most famous tales associated with Anusuya is her test by the Trinity—Brahma, Vishnu, and Shiva. According to the legend:

1.	The divine trio, intrigued by her devotion, decided to test her virtue.

2.	Disguised as mendicants, they approached her hermitage while Sage Atri was away and requested alms. However, they added a peculiar condition: she had to serve them food without wearing clothes.

3.	Without hesitation, Anusuya prayed to her inner strength and transformed the three gods into infants, thus preserving her chastity. She then served them with motherly love and affection.

4.	Pleased with her virtue, the trio revealed their true forms and blessed her. They also granted her the boon of giving birth to the incarnation of all three gods, in the form of her son, Dattatreya.

Role as a Mother

Anusuya and Sage Atri were blessed with three illustrious sons, each an embodiment of divinity:

- **Dattatreya:** The combined incarnation of Brahma, Vishnu, and Shiva. He became a great sage and teacher, spreading the principles of renunciation and spirituality.

- **Durvasa:** An incarnation of Lord Shiva, known for his temper and deep commitment to dharma.

- **Chandra (Soma):** A partial incarnation of Brahma, revered as the Moon God in Hindu tradition.

Through her nurturing and guidance, Anusuya shaped their spiritual and moral values, contributing significantly to their divine missions.

Philosophical and Spiritual Contributions of Anusuya

Anusuya was not merely a devoted wife and mother but also a spiritual beacon in her own right. She dedicated her life to the service of humanity, teaching the values of truth, compassion, and humility. She established her ashram with Atri in the serene forests near the Chitrakoot region, where they guided seekers on the path of righteousness.

Her selfless acts of charity, including feeding the hungry, healing the sick, and offering refuge to travelers, made her ashram a center of solace and learning. She also taught the importance of adhering to dharma, emphasizing the balance between worldly duties and spiritual pursuits.

Encounter with Sita and Rama

Anusuya plays a pivotal role in the Ramayana during Lord Rama's exile. When Rama, Sita, and Lakshmana visited her hermitage in Chitrakoot, Anusuya welcomed them with great hospitality. She provided invaluable advice to Sita, sharing wisdom about the duties and virtues of an ideal wife.

Moved by her devotion, Sita sought Anusuya's blessings and guidance. Anusuya gifted Sita celestial garments and ornaments that never withered or tarnished, symbolizing the enduring nature of true virtue and devotion.

Legacy

Anusuya's life remains an inspiring saga of love, devotion, and spiritual strength. Her unwavering adherence to dharma and her ability to overcome challenges with grace and wisdom continue to be celebrated in Hindu culture.

In honor of her contributions, the **Anusuya Ashram** near Chitrakoot stands as a testament to her legacy. Pilgrims visit this site to pay homage to her virtues and seek her blessings.

Anusuya's story teaches us the importance of humility, resilience, and the power of devotion in overcoming adversities. She is revered not only as the devoted wife of Sage Atri but also as a spiritual luminary who shaped the moral and spiritual fabric of her time.

7. Sumitra

Sumitra, Lakshmana's mother and Dasharatha's second wife, is often overshadowed by Kaushalya and Kaikeyi in the epic. However, her role was critical in shaping Lakshmana's character and his unwavering loyalty to Rama. When Rama was exiled, Sumitra selflessly encouraged Lakshmana to accompany his brother, reminding him of his duty and the importance of dharma. Sumitra's quiet strength and acceptance of her son's sacrifices make her a poignant example of maternal resilience and wisdom.

8. Shrutakirti

Shrutakirti, the youngest of Janaka's four daughters, married Rama's youngest brother, Shatrughna. Although her presence is minimal in the epic, Shrutakirti represents the unity and harmony within Rama's extended family. Her role complements the theme of familial bonds, and her quiet dedication to her husband mirrors Sita's virtues. Shrutakirti's character is a reminder of the understated yet essential roles of women in ensuring familial stability.

9. Kaushalya

Kaushalya, Rama's mother and Dasharatha's chief queen, embodies patience and grace. Although deeply hurt by her son's exile, she accepted it with dignity, understanding the greater purpose behind it. Kaushalya's silent suffering and unwavering faith in

Rama highlight the emotional sacrifices of mothers in maintaining dharma. Her character portrays the strength required to endure personal loss for the greater good, making her a timeless figure of maternal love and resilience.

Kaushalya is often portrayed as a dignified and loving figure in the Ramayana. Her life is a testament to patience, righteousness, and maternal devotion, embodying the ideals of motherhood and dharma. While her character is not as extensively explored as others, piecing together her journey offers a profound glimpse into her role before and after Rama's birth and her influence during his upbringing and adulthood.

Before the Birth of Rama

Kaushalya, the daughter of King Sukaushal and queen of the Kosala kingdom, was born into royalty. Her upbringing in a prosperous and dharmic household shaped her into a compassionate and virtuous individual. As the eldest princess of Kosala, she was well-versed in the scriptures, skilled in managing a royal household, and deeply devout.

When she married King Dasharatha, she became his senior queen, bringing grace and wisdom to the royal palace of Ayodhya. Kaushalya's marriage to Dasharatha was harmonious initially, and her position as the primary queen brought her respect and influence. However, with the arrival of Dasharatha's two other queens, Kaikeyi and Sumitra, Kaushalya had to adjust to sharing her husband's attention and affection.

Despite her status as the senior queen, Kaushalya experienced emotional challenges due to Dasharatha's preference for Kaikeyi. This dynamic created an undercurrent of sadness in her life, but Kaushalya remained dignified and focused on her duties. Her greatest sorrow during this period was her inability to bear a child, a situation that weighed heavily on her and Dasharatha.

After the Birth of Rama

The birth of Rama brought immense joy and fulfillment to Kaushalya's life. His arrival was seen as a divine blessing, and her role as his mother elevated her status in the palace and in Ayodhya. Kaushalya was deeply devoted to her son, seeing him as not only her child but also as an embodiment of dharma and divinity.

Kausalya's love for Rama was evident in her care and dedication. She personally oversaw his upbringing, instilling in him values of righteousness, compassion, and humility. Her influence played a crucial role in shaping Rama's character, and she took pride in his wisdom and ability to win the affection of everyone around him.

While she loved Rama unconditionally, Kaushalya did not neglect her duties toward her stepsons, Bharata, Lakshmana, and Shatrughna. She treated them with maternal affection, fostering harmony among the brothers. Her nurturing presence ensured that the royal household remained a place of love and unity.

Bringing Up Rama

Kaushalya's parenting style combined warmth with a strong emphasis on dharma. She ensured that Rama received the best education, both in scriptures and martial arts. Her lessons were not limited to academic or physical training but extended to practical wisdom and emotional strength. Through stories and personal example, she taught him the importance of compassion, selflessness, and respect for elders.

Kausalya's bond with Rama was unique. She often acted as his confidante, offering guidance and emotional support. Her encouragement and belief in his abilities gave Rama the confidence to face challenges with grace and courage. She celebrated his successes and comforted him in times of difficulty, embodying the ideal of a supportive and nurturing mother.

During Rama's Adulthood

As Rama grew into adulthood, Kaushalya's pride in him deepened. She rejoiced in his marriage to Sita, seeing the union as a divine match. Kaushalya's wisdom and experience made her an important advisor in the palace, particularly in matters concerning her son and his future role as king.

However, her life took a dramatic turn when Kaikeyi demanded the exile of Rama and the coronation of her son Bharata. Kaushalya was devastated by this decision, seeing it as both a personal betrayal and a violation of dharma. Her grief was profound, but she maintained her composure, drawing strength from her faith in Rama's virtues.

Kaushalya's emotional struggle during this period is one of the most poignant aspects of her story. She tried to reason with Dasharatha, pleading for justice for her son, but her efforts were in vain. Despite her sorrow, she supported Rama's decision to honor his father's promise to Kaikeyi, recognizing his commitment to dharma. Her parting words to Rama were filled with both maternal love and spiritual wisdom, urging him to remain steadfast in his principles.

Her Role in the Lives of Her Children

Kaushalya's influence had extended beyond Rama. As the senior queen and mother figure, she played a significant role in the lives of Bharata, Lakshmana, and Shatrughna. Her nurturing nature and fairness ensured that the brothers grew up in an atmosphere of love and mutual respect.

Even during the years of Rama's exile, Kaushalya's presence in the palace provided a sense of stability. She became a source of solace for Sita and a moral anchor for the royal family. Her interactions with Bharata after Dasharatha's death highlight her magnanimity and ability to forgive. She supported Bharata's decision to rule as Rama's regent, seeing it as an act of devotion and loyalty.

Her Later Years

Kaushalya's later years were marked by the joy of Rama's return to Ayodhya and his coronation as king. She witnessed the restoration of dharma and the prosperity of the kingdom under her son's rule. Her love for her grandchildren and her continued role as a guide and matriarch in the palace reflected her enduring strength and wisdom.

Kaushalya's life is a testament to patience, devotion, and resilience. As a mother, queen, and woman, she navigated the complexities of palace life with grace, leaving a legacy of love and dharma that resonates through the Ramayana. Her story reminds us of the silent strength of women who, through their wisdom and compassion, shape the destinies of their families and kingdoms.

10. Sulochana

Sulochana, the wife of Ravana's son Indrajit, is a tragic figure whose loyalty to her husband and dharma shines through her brief appearance in the Ramayana. She mourned Indrajit's death but refrained from cursing

Rama, recognizing his adherence to dharma. Sulochana's quiet dignity and understanding of dharma reflect the complexity of grief and acceptance, adding emotional depth to the epic.

11. Vindhyavasini

Vindhyavasini, a goddess residing in the Vindhya mountains, is briefly mentioned as a protector of sages and travelers. Her subtle interventions and blessings ensured safety for Rama and his companions during their journey. Vindhyavasini symbolizes divine support and the role of nature deities in facilitating the epic's progression.

12. Surpanakha

Surpanakha is a central figure in the *Ramayana*, particularly in the narrative of the events leading to the abduction of Sita. She is a rakshasi (demoness) and the sister of Ravana, the king of Lanka. Her story is often overshadowed by her infamous role in the Ramayana, but her life and motivations reveal much about the complex interplay of family dynamics, love, revenge, and fate. Below is a detailed account of Surpanakha's life, highlighting her background, her significant actions, and the consequences of her choices.

Background and Lineage

Surpanakha was born to the sage Vishrava and a rakshasi woman, *Kaikasi*, who was Ravana's mother.

Vishrava, a revered sage, married Kaikasi, and together they had several children, including Ravana, Kumbhakarna, Vibhishana, and Surpanakha. Surpanakha's siblings were all powerful figures in the *Ramayana*, with Ravana being the central antagonist.

Surpanakha's name itself has symbolic meaning: "Surpanakha" translates to "having sharp nails," which is often interpreted as a reflection of her aggressive, fiery nature. She is depicted as a fierce, powerful being, often disregarding the norms of the world around her. Despite her somewhat marginalized position in the larger mythological narrative, her story is important in the buildup to the central conflict between Rama and Ravana.

Her Role in the Ramayana

The Encounter with Rama

Surpanakha first appears in the *Ramayana* after Rama, Sita, and Lakshmana are living in exile in the forest. The trio arrives in the Dandaka forest, a vast and desolate wilderness, where Surpanakha first encounters them. As she sees the handsome and noble-looking Rama, she is immediately attracted to him and desires him as her husband. She approaches him and proposes marriage, but Rama, bound by his commitment to Sita, rejects her advances politely. He directs her to his brother Lakshmana, hoping that he will handle the situation.

Surpanakha, finding Lakshmana equally attractive, turns to him with the same proposition. However, Lakshmana, though younger and equally handsome, also rejects her, mocking her for attempting to seduce both brothers. Feeling humiliated, Surpanakha becomes enraged and decides to take revenge on Sita, whom she views as the obstacle to her desires.

The Attack on Sita

Surpanakha's rejection turns into an obsession. In a fit of jealousy and anger, she transforms herself into a terrifying, monstrous form and attempts to kill Sita. She hopes to take Sita's place by force, eliminating the woman who is the object of both Rama's and Lakshmana's affections. However, her attack is thwarted by Lakshmana, who, following Rama's command, cuts off Surpanakha's nose and ears in an act of self-defense and protection of Sita.

The mutilation of Surpanakha becomes a pivotal moment in the *Ramayana*. Humiliated and in pain, Surpanakha retreats to her brother Ravana, seeking revenge and inciting his anger. This act of vengeance sets off a chain of events that eventually leads to the kidnapping of Sita.

The Aftermath: Revenge and the Kidnapping of Sita

Surpanakha's mutilation by Lakshmana is a turning point in the narrative. With her wounded ego and her desire for revenge, Surpanakha goes to Ravana and describes Rama's beauty, valor, and his devotion to his wife. She tells Ravana about the enchanting Sita and how she is an obstacle to her own desires. Surpanakha urges Ravana to kidnap Sita and bring her to Lanka, hoping to ruin Rama's happiness and cause further suffering.

Motivated by his sister's plea and his own lust for Sita, Ravana devises a plan to abduct her. With the help of the golden deer (*maricha*), he distracts Rama and Lakshmana, leaving Sita alone. Ravana, in the guise of a hermit, tricks Sita into stepping outside their hut, and he kidnaps her, whisking her away to Lanka.

Surpanakha's Role in Ravana's Downfall

Although Surpanakha's desire to take revenge on Sita directly leads to Sita's abduction, it is important to understand that her actions have far-reaching consequences. Ravana's kidnapping of Sita sets the stage for the epic battle between the forces of good, led by Rama, and the forces of evil, represented by Ravana and his army. The war that follows eventually leads to Ravana's death and the restoration of dharma.

However, Surpanakha's actions are also symbolic of a larger theme in the *Ramayana*—the destructive nature of unrequited desire and unchecked revenge. Her decision to cause suffering out of jealousy and her inability to control her emotions ultimately leads to the downfall of her family. While Surpanakha is not directly involved in the war itself, her impulsive actions play a significant role in the escalation of the conflict.

Character Traits and Symbolism

Surpanakha embodies the raw, unchecked emotional impulses of desire, jealousy, and vengeance. She represents a force of nature that disrupts the harmony and peace of the world around her. Her story in the *Ramayana* is a cautionary tale about the destructive consequences of obsessive love, jealousy, and revenge.

•	**Unrequited Love**: Surpanakha's desire for Rama and later Lakshmana is not reciprocated. Her response to this rejection, turning into an obsessive and destructive desire for revenge, speaks to the dangers of unrequited love.

•	**Jealousy and Revenge**: Her jealousy toward Sita transforms into hatred and a vengeful spirit. Surpanakha's story highlights the destructive potential of jealousy, a negative emotion that drives individuals to irrational actions.

•	**Transformation and Power**: Surpanakha's ability to change shape—whether through physical transformation or her emotional volatility—emphasizes her connection to the rakshasa (demon) world, where beings can shape-shift and manipulate reality for personal gain.

•	**Mutilation and Humiliation**: Her physical mutilation, losing her nose and ears, becomes a symbol of how her unchecked emotions and actions have left her humiliated. This transformation reflects her inner state of chaos and dishonor.

Surpanakha's Legacy

Surpanakha's life, marked by unrequited love, revenge, and the desire for power, is central to the events of the *Ramayana* and its moral lessons. Though her role is relatively brief, her actions are pivotal in igniting the chain of events that lead to the war between Rama and Ravana. Surpanakha's story serves as a reminder of the destructive potential of unchecked emotions and the consequences of acting out of revenge.

In the larger context of the *Ramayana*, Surpanakha is a symbol of how personal dissatisfaction and emotional turmoil can ripple out and affect not only the individual but the entire world around them. While her tale is tragic, it also emphasizes the importance of wisdom, self-restraint, and the need to temper emotional impulses in the pursuit of harmony and dharma.

13. Aditi

Aditi is a significant figure in Hindu mythology, especially in the *Vedas* and *Ramayana*, known as the mother of the Adityas, the celestial beings or solar deities who represent various divine forces. Aditi's role and her association with the Adityas play a crucial part in Vedic cosmology and the balance of cosmic forces.

Here's a deeper look into Aditi, her sons, and the significance of the Adityas:

Aditi: The Divine Mother

Aditi, in Vedic literature, is regarded as a primal goddess, often symbolizing the boundless, infinite, and nurturing aspects of the universe. She is considered the mother of the gods and one of the daughters of Daksha, one of the ancient sages. Aditi's marriage to Sage Kashyapa, a revered sage, led to the birth of several divine and celestial beings, including the Adityas.

Attributes of Aditi

•   **Motherhood and Cosmic Balance**: Aditi is often depicted as the embodiment of motherhood, peace, and cosmic harmony. She is seen as the source of all that is nourishing and life-giving, both in the physical world and the spiritual realm.

•   **Symbol of Infinity and Freedom**: The name *Aditi* is derived from the root "a" meaning "not" and "diti" meaning "bound" or "limited," which indicates her nature as limitless and free from constraint. She represents the vastness of the universe and is often associated with the sun and the infinite.

•   **Role in Creation**: As the mother of many deities, Aditi is a key figure in the Vedic creation myths. She is seen as a nurturer, providing for the growth and balance of the cosmos, particularly through her sons, the Adityas, who uphold divine order.

The Adityas: Sons of Aditi

The Adityas are a group of twelve deities, each representing an aspect of the cosmic order and contributing to the functioning of the universe. They are considered the sons of Aditi and Kashyapa, and each one governs a specific aspect of life or the natural world. The Adityas are primarily solar deities, and their collective role is to sustain the cosmic and moral order (*rta*).

List of the Twelve Adityas

While the list of the Adityas varies across different texts, the most commonly accepted twelve are:

1.   **Varuna**: The god of the cosmic law, water, and the ocean, representing moral and cosmic order.

2.   **Mitra**: The god of friendship, contracts, and the sun, often associated with light and truth.

3.   **Aryaman**: The god of hospitality and the protector of those who are traveling or in need.

4.   **Bhaga**: The god of wealth, fortune, and marital happiness.

5.   **Vivasvan** (Surya): The sun god, representing light, truth, and the life-giving force of the universe.

6.   **Dhatri**: The god associated with the act of creation and the sustainer of life.

7.   **Indra**: The king of gods, god of rain, storms, and war, who upholds the world's vitality and vigor.

8.   **Pushan**: The god of nourishment, agriculture, and the protector of travelers.

9.   **Tvashta**: The god of artisans, crafts, and architecture, responsible for the creation of weapons and structures.

10.   **Savitar**: The god of the sun, light, and motion, often considered a synonym for the sun's rays.

11.   **Parjanya**: The god of rain, thunder, and the storms, important for agricultural growth.

12.   **Amsa**: One of the lesser-known Adityas, representing a fragment or part of a larger divine force.

These twelve Adityas represent the totality of life, from the sun's power to natural elements like water, air, and fire. They are responsible for maintaining the laws of nature and supporting the cycle of life, ensuring balance in the universe.

Role and Significance of the Adityas

1.   **Cosmic and Moral Order**: The Adityas play a vital role in sustaining the moral and cosmic order (*rta*). As deities associated with various aspects of creation, they maintain balance in the world, ensuring that the cycles of nature and life run smoothly.

2.   **Solar Deities**: Since many of the Adityas are closely connected with the sun, they are often depicted as solar deities who control the movement of the sun, light, and heat. This connection to the sun is symbolic

of truth, knowledge, and the eradication of darkness, both physical and spiritual.

3.   **Protectors of Dharma**: Each of the Adityas governs a particular aspect of life that is essential for the welfare of the world. By performing their duties, they ensure that dharma (righteousness) is upheld. For example, Varuna governs cosmic law, Mitra governs friendship and truth, and Vivasvan (Surya) represents vitality and truth through his association with light.

4.   **Support for the Gods and Humanity**: The Adityas are instrumental in the protection and support of both divine beings and humans. They act as intermediaries between the gods and humanity, offering blessings, protection, and guidance.

5.   **Symbol of the Sun's Power**: The twelve Adityas are often considered the different phases or manifestations of the sun's rays. Their names and attributes often mirror the changing positions of the sun, from dawn to noon to dusk.

Aditi and the Birth of Lord Rama

Aditi's most significant connection to the Ramayana comes through her son Vivasvan, who is associated with Surya, the sun god. In some versions of the story, Lord Rama is described as being a descendant of Surya (through his ancestor, Ikshvaku). Thus, Aditi's influence is felt in the Ramayana, as her divine children play a crucial role in the lineage that leads to Rama.

Aditi's Contribution to the Universe

Aditi is revered as the ultimate divine mother, who not only bore the Adityas but also nurtured them into being powerful cosmic forces. Her essence is tied to the sustenance of the universe and its creation, preservation, and dissolution. As a mother, she exemplifies the nurturing power of the divine, ensuring that her sons—the Adityas—fulfill their respective roles in maintaining the universe's balance.

Aditi in the Vedas and Upanishads

In the Vedic texts, Aditi is also associated with *Aditi hymns* in the *Rigveda*, where she is described as a cosmic mother who is connected with the heavens, supporting all creatures in the universe. In the *Upanishads*, she is sometimes regarded as the embodiment of the *Brahman* (the ultimate reality), symbolizing the mother of all beings, from the celestial to the terrestrial.

Aditi is an essential figure in Hindu mythology, both in the *Ramayana* and the broader Vedic tradition. As the mother of the twelve Adityas, she represents the limitless, nurturing, and sustaining forces of the universe. The Adityas, in turn, symbolize various aspects of life, from natural elements to moral principles, and are integral to the cosmic order. Aditi's influence spans beyond the *Ramayana*, with her presence felt throughout Hindu scriptures, where she stands as a symbol of the divine feminine energy that nurtures all forms of existence.

14. Vedavati

Vedavati is a significant yet often overlooked figure in Hindu mythology and the *Ramayana*. She is depicted as a woman of extraordinary spiritual strength, asceticism, and wisdom. Her life story is filled with deep emotions, a commitment to her vows, and a connection to divine justice that extends beyond her mortal existence. Below is a detailed account of Vedavati's life, deeds, and her spiritual significance, along with a discussion of other prominent women sages in Hindu tradition.

The Life of Vedavati

Vedavati was a highly revered sage, known for her extreme devotion to spirituality and her unshakable commitment to her vows. Her story is primarily found in the *Ramayana* and certain other texts like the *Mahabharata* and Puranas. The narrative of Vedavati's life is deeply intertwined with themes of chastity, asceticism, and sacrifice.

Her Birth and Early Life

Vedavati was born as the daughter of a great sage, *Kashyapa*, or sometimes mentioned as the daughter of *Brahma*, the creator god, depending on the text. Her early life is marked by a strong spiritual inclination, as she was committed to pursuing a life of devotion, meditation, and ascetic practices. As a child, she was already recognized for her great intelligence, wisdom, and spiritual energy.

She was also described as extremely beautiful, which played a central role in her story. Vedavati's beauty attracted the attention of *Ravana*, the powerful and tenacious king of Lanka. Ravana, known for his lust and arrogance, was enamored by Vedavati's appearance and made advances toward her, desiring to marry her. Vedavati, however, was committed to her vow of celibacy and to her spiritual practices. She rejected Ravana's advances, which infuriated him.

Ravana's Attempt and Vedavati's Vow

Ravana's rejection was not taken lightly. In a fit of rage and desire, Ravana attempted to force himself upon Vedavati. In response to this violation, Vedavati made a powerful vow of revenge. She swore to purify herself through extreme penance, and to rid Ravana of his arrogance and pride. As part of her vow, she vowed to end her life through self-immolation if Ravana continued to pursue her, but she also promised that she would be reborn with the sole purpose of destroying Ravana.

After Ravana's attempt to force her, Vedavati entered the fire (a practice known as *Agni Pariksha*) and immolated herself, hoping to purify her soul and eliminate the evil forces of Ravana. Her self-sacrifice in the fire was symbolic of her renunciation of worldly desires and her ultimate commitment to justice and dharma.

Rebirth and Connection with Sita

The story of Vedavati's rebirth is one of the key aspects of her life. It is believed that Vedavati was reborn as *Sita*, the wife of Lord Rama, after her self-immolation. In this new birth, she fulfilled her vow by being born as the daughter of King Janaka. In the Ramayana, Ravana's desire to abduct Sita is ultimately the catalyst that leads to his downfall, fulfilling Vedavati's vow of revenge against him. This connection between Vedavati and Sita is often drawn to show how Vedavati's life and asceticism were intertwined with the divine purpose of restoring dharma and justice.

Vedavati's Role in the Ramayana

While Vedavati's direct role in the *Ramayana* is not as prominent as Sita's, her presence looms large in the background. Her story is often viewed as an important precursor to the events that lead to Ravana's downfall. Vedavati represents the power of spiritual purity and the strength of vows in the face of adversity. Her rejection of Ravana's advances, followed by her self-sacrifice and rebirth as Sita, underscores the themes of devotion, sacrifice, and the role of divine will in shaping destiny.

Chapter Six - Insignificant Warriors

1. Angada

Angada, the son of Vali and Tara, was a young yet formidable warrior in the Vanara army. Despite his father's death at Rama's hands, Angada displayed unwavering loyalty and bravery. He played a pivotal role in the search for Sita and acted as a messenger to Ravana, urging him to surrender. His resilience during battles and diplomatic attempts showcased his maturity, proving that even younger warriors could make significant contributions.

Angad, a pivotal character in the *Ramayana*, is a vanara prince whose life is a story of transformation, strength, loyalty, and wisdom. He is remembered for his remarkable role in Lord Rama's mission to rescue Sita and for his exemplary display of leadership, courage, and devotion. Below is a comprehensive account of Angad's life, powers, spiritual knowledge, and illustrious career.

Early Life and Parentage

- **Birth and Lineage**: Angad was born to **Vali**, the mighty king of Kishkindha, and **Tara**, one of the most intelligent and politically astute women in the *Ramayana*. As the son of Vali, Angad inherited immense physical strength and fighting prowess. From his mother, he gained intelligence, diplomatic skills, and a deep understanding of dharma.

- **Youthful Aspirations**: Being the crown prince of Kishkindha, Angad was groomed to succeed his father. However, his father's duel with Lord Rama, resulting in Vali's death, drastically altered Angad's life path.

Challenges After Vali's Death

- **Emotional Turmoil**: After Vali's death at the hands of Lord Rama, Angad faced an identity crisis. He initially felt bitterness and resentment toward Rama but was guided by his mother Tara and Hanuman to see the larger picture of dharma.

- **Acceptance of Sugriva's Rule**: Sugriva, Vali's brother, became the king of Kishkindha, and Angad, despite being the rightful heir, accepted Sugriva's authority. This showed his maturity and willingness to prioritize unity over personal ambitions.

Angad's Powers and Skills

- **Extraordinary Physical Strength**: Angad inherited his father's legendary strength. He could leap great distances, defeat mighty foes, and endure extreme physical challenges, making him one of the strongest vanaras.

- **Combat Prowess**: He was a skilled warrior, adept in hand-to-hand combat and the use of vanara-style tactics. His agility and reflexes were unmatched.

- **Immovable Resolve**: Angad's most iconic moment showcasing his strength was when he planted his foot in Ravana's court and challenged anyone to move it. This act symbolized his indomitable spirit and physical might.

Spiritual Knowledge and Dharma

•   **Guided by Wise Mentors**: Angad grew under the tutelage of his mother Tara, Lord Hanuman, and eventually Lord Rama. These influences molded his understanding of dharma, duty, and devotion.

•   **Commitment to Righteousness**: Despite personal losses, Angad aligned himself with Lord Rama's mission, showing his ability to rise above individual grievances for a greater cause.

•   **Diplomatic Eloquence**: Angad's role as an envoy to Ravana highlighted his ability to articulate the principles of dharma and appeal to the moral conscience of his adversary.

Role in Rama's Mission

Search for Sita

•   **Integral to the Search Party**: Angad was part of the elite group of vanaras led by Hanuman to locate Sita. His leadership and unwavering determination kept the team motivated during their arduous journey.

•   **Crossing the Ocean**: Alongside Hanuman, Jambavan, and other vanaras, Angad was pivotal in strategizing how to cross the ocean to reach Lanka.

War in Lanka

•   **Fighting Ravana's Forces**: Angad displayed unparalleled courage during the battle of Lanka, facing formidable foes such as Indrajit, Kumbhakarna, and other rakshasas.

- **Diplomatic Mission to Ravana**: Before the war began, Angad was sent to Ravana's court as an emissary. His fearless demeanor, logical arguments, and challenge to Ravana's warriors to move his planted foot showcased his strength, intelligence, and dedication to peace before war.

Angad as a Leader

- **Crown Prince of Kishkindha**: After the war, Angad was appointed the crown prince by Lord Rama. This marked the continuation of Vali's lineage and recognized Angad's contributions to the mission.

- **Mentorship Role**: Angad likely became a mentor for the younger generation of vanaras, teaching them the values of dharma, leadership, and service.

Angad's Personal Transformation

- **From Anger to Devotion**: Angad's initial resentment toward Rama transformed into unwavering loyalty and devotion. His spiritual growth is evident in his ability to forgive and focus on the greater good.

- **A Bridge Between Families**: Angad's acceptance of Sugriva's rule helped bridge the divide between Vali's and Sugriva's factions within the vanara kingdom, ensuring unity in Kishkindha.

Legacy

• **Model of Loyalty**: Angad's dedication to Lord Rama and the mission to rescue Sita made him a symbol of loyalty and righteousness.

• **Symbol of Courage**: His actions in Ravana's court and on the battlefield demonstrated his physical and moral courage.

• **Diplomatic Wisdom**: Angad's eloquence and diplomacy in dealing with adversaries showed his intelligence and understanding of dharma.

Angad's life is a tale of resilience, transformation, and devotion. Despite personal tragedies, he rose to the occasion, playing a crucial role in Lord Rama's mission. As a warrior, diplomat, and spiritual figure, Angad embodied the ideals of dharma, loyalty, and leadership, leaving an indelible mark on the *Ramayana*.

2. Jambavan

The elder among the Vanaras, Jambavan was a wise and seasoned fighter who aided Rama's army with his strategies. Though not directly involved in significant combat; his wisdom and encouragement to Hanuman to recall his strength during the search for Sita played a critical role. His guidance exemplified the importance of experience in warfare.

Jambavan: The Wise King of Bears

Jambavan, the King of Bears, is a central figure in the Ramayana, known for his wisdom, experience, and strategic mind. Created by Lord Brahma, Jambavan is one of the oldest beings in the epic. He is said to have witnessed the churning of the ocean (Samudra Manthan) and possesses immense knowledge and strength despite his advanced age.

Qualities and Characteristics:

1. **Wisdom and Knowledge**: Jambavan is revered for his profound understanding of dharma and his ability to advise others in moments of crisis. His sagacious counsel often guides others in critical situations.

2. **Loyalty and Devotion**: A devoted follower of Lord Rama, Jambavan's unwavering faith in dharma motivates his every action.

3. **Physical Strength and Agility**: Though aged, Jambavan retains remarkable physical prowess.

4. **Diplomatic Skills**: He plays the role of a mediator, offering insightful suggestions during pivotal moments.

Life and Role in the Ramayana:

Jambavan plays a crucial role in the search for Sita and the battle against Ravana. When Hanuman momentarily forgets his immense abilities, Jambavan reminds him of his latent powers and motivates him to perform his legendary leap across the ocean to Lanka. This act underscores Jambavan's ability to inspire and mobilize his allies, ensuring the success of Rama's mission.

During the battle in Lanka, Jambavan participates actively, rallying the Vanara army and fighting valiantly against Ravana's forces. His strategic acumen and encouragement bolster morale and ensure that Rama's forces stay united and focused.

Contribution to the Epic:

Jambavan's role as a motivator and guide cannot be understated. By inspiring Hanuman to leap to Lanka, he catalyzes a chain of events that leads to Sita's discovery and eventual rescue. His wise counsel often acts as the moral compass for the Vanara warriors, ensuring that their actions align with dharma.

Legacy:

Jambavan's legacy extends beyond the Ramayana. He is a recurring figure in other texts, such as the Mahabharata, where he plays a role in Krishna obtaining the Syamantaka jewel. His character symbolizes the wisdom and strength that come with age and experience, making him a revered figure in Hindu mythology.

3. Nala

Nala, a Vanara engineer, was instrumental in constructing the bridge (Rama Setu) across the ocean to Lanka. His skills in engineering turned the tide of the war, enabling Rama's army to invade Ravana's stronghold. Though his role was not as pronounced on the battlefield, his contribution was vital to the epic's progression.

4. Neela

Neela, another Vanara warrior, served as the commander-in-chief of Rama's army. Known for his strength and leadership, he played a crucial role in organizing the troops during the battle against Ravana's forces. His strategic insights and combat skills showcased the discipline within the Vanara ranks.

5. Sugriva: The Vanara King

Though a more prominent figure than others on this list, Sugriva's martial contributions are often overshadowed by his leadership. Once exiled by Vali, he regained his kingdom with Rama's help and became a loyal ally. His courage and skill as a warrior were evident in the final battle.

Sugriva, the Vanara king, is a pivotal character in the Ramayana. Estranged from his elder brother, Vali, Sugriva initially struggles to reclaim his kingdom of Kishkindha but later becomes an ally of Rama in his quest to rescue Sita.

Qualities and Characteristics:

1.   **Bravery**: Sugriva demonstrates courage in confronting Vali with Rama's assistance and later leading the Vanara army against Ravana.

2.   **Loyalty**: Once his alliance with Rama is established, Sugriva becomes a steadfast supporter of Rama's cause.

3.   **Diplomacy**: Sugriva is skilled in forging alliances, as seen in his pact with Rama.

4.   **Flawed but Redeemable**: Sugriva initially falters in fulfilling his promise to assist Rama but redeems himself through his later actions.

Life and Role in the Ramayana:

Sugriva's life is marked by a tragic conflict with his brother Vali. Banished from Kishkindha, he lives in exile until he encounters Rama and Lakshmana. Their alliance is cemented by Rama's promise to help Sugriva reclaim his throne in exchange for assistance in finding Sita.

After Vali's death, Sugriva ascends the throne and fulfills his promise by mobilizing the Vanara army to search for Sita. His leadership during the campaign against Ravana showcases his abilities as a king and warrior.

Contribution to the Epic:

Sugriva's contributions are instrumental in Rama's success. His army's efforts lead to the discovery of Sita and the eventual victory over Ravana. Sugriva exemplifies the importance of loyalty and redemption, illustrating how personal shortcomings can be overcome through dedication to a noble cause.

Legacy:

Sugriva's story serves as a reminder of the value of alliances and the potential for redemption. His role in the Ramayana highlights the transformative power of trust and collaboration in overcoming adversity.

6. Indrajit (Meghnad): The Formidable Warrior Prince of Ramayana

Indrajit, Ravana's son, was a powerful and cunning warrior. His mastery of dark magic and his use of the Brahmastra showcased his prowess on the battlefield. Despite his eventual defeat, Indrajit's skill made him one of Rama's most formidable foes, adding tension to the narrative.

Indrajit, also known as Meghnad, is one of the most intriguing and powerful characters in the Ramayana. As the eldest son of Ravana, the demon king of Lanka, Indrajit's life is a tale of unmatched valor, devotion to family, and adherence to the demonic path of adharma. His exploits and ultimate demise are crucial to the unfolding of the epic's events. A complex figure, Indrajit exemplifies both the heights of prowess and the tragic consequences of aligning with unrighteousness.

Birth and Early Life

Indrajit was born to Ravana and Mandodari, the queen of Lanka, and his birth was marked by auspicious signs foretelling his great destiny. As the crown prince of Lanka, he was groomed from an early age to be a warrior and heir. His education included mastery of weapons, warfare, and the sacred Vedic sciences, reflecting his dual identity as both a scholar and a warrior.

Indrajit's brilliance as a warrior became evident early in his life. Under the tutelage of Shukracharya, the guru of the Rakshasas, he mastered celestial weapons (astras) and earned proficiency in both military strategy and the dark arts of sorcery. He also gained knowledge of yajnas (sacrificial rituals), which he would later use to invoke divine powers during battles.

The Origin of the Name "Indrajit"

Indrajit's fame was cemented when he defeated Indra, the king of the gods, in battle. According to legend, Ravana sought to subjugate the heavens, and Indrajit played a pivotal role in the campaign. With his mastery of celestial weapons, he overwhelmed Indra and captured him, imprisoning the king of the gods in Lanka.

This incredible feat earned him the name 'Indrajit,' meaning 'Conqueror of Indra.' His father, Ravana, praised him as the mightiest warrior in the three worlds and celebrated his unparalleled prowess. However, this victory also sowed the seeds of his eventual downfall, as his triumph over Indra brought him into direct opposition with the forces of dharma.

Indrajit's Role in the War of Lanka

Indrajit emerges as one of the most significant antagonists in the Ramayana during the war of Lanka. His unmatched skill in battle, cunning strategies, and mastery of divine weaponry make him a formidable foe for Rama and his allies. Indrajit's contributions to the war are marked by both extraordinary victories and acts of treachery.

1. Victory with the Nagapasha Weapon

During the initial stages of war, Indrajit demonstrated his fearsome power by using the Nagapasha, a celestial weapon that bound Rama and Lakshmana with serpentine coils. This left the brothers immobilized and vulnerable, nearly costing them their lives. It was only through the intervention of Garuda, the eagle mount of Vishnu, that they were freed from the weapon's grip.

2. Illusion and Deception in Battle

Indrajit's use of sorcery and illusions in warfare set him apart as a unique adversary. He frequently employed invisibility and other deceptive tactics to gain the upper hand. His mastery of the Mayavi art of illusion allowed him to confound his enemies and strike fear into their hearts.

3. The Illusion of Sita's Death

One of Indrajit's most infamous acts was his creation of an illusion in which he appeared to kill Sita. By conjuring a false image of Sita and slaying it before Hanuman and the Vanara army, Indrajit sought to demoralize Rama's forces. This act temporarily succeeded in sowing despair among the allies until the truth of the illusion was revealed.

4. Battle with Lakshmana and the Yajna of Power

Indrajit's most significant encounter occurred when he faced Lakshmana in battle. Before this confrontation, he attempted to perform a yajna (sacrificial ritual) in the sanctuary of Nikumbhila to gain invincibility. Guided by Bibhishan, Rama's ally and Ravana's estranged brother, Lakshmana disrupted the ritual, forcing Indrajit to confront him prematurely.

In the ensuing battle, Indrajit fought fiercely, demonstrating his unmatched skills with celestial weapons. However, Lakshmana, empowered by Rama's blessings and guided by dharma, ultimately vanquished Indrajit with the Brahmastra, a divine weapon. Indrajit's death marked a turning point in the war, depriving Ravana of his most potent defender and hastening the fall of Lanka.

Indrajit's Qualities and Attributes

1. Unparalleled Warrior

Indrajit's mastery of divine weapons made him one of the most formidable warriors in the Ramayana. He wielded weapons granted by the gods, including the Brahmastra and the Nagapasha, and was adept at both physical combat and strategic warfare. His ability to fight while invisible added an unprecedented dimension to his combat style.

2. Devotion to Family

Despite his alignment with adharma, Indrajit's loyalty to his father, Ravana, was unwavering. He fought not only as a warrior but also as a devoted son, willing to sacrifice his life to uphold his father's honor and defend Lanka.

3. Arrogance and Overconfidence

Indrajit's victories and his belief in his invincibility often led to hubris. His overconfidence, particularly during the yajna at Nikumbhila, proved to be his undoing, as he underestimated the determination and skill of Lakshmana.

4. Complex Morality

While Indrajit's actions were often driven by adharma, his devotion to his family and his adherence to the warrior's code added layers to his character. He embodies the duality of a noble warrior who aligns himself with an unrighteous cause, highlighting the moral complexities of the Ramayana.

Contribution to the Ramayana

Indrajit's role in the Ramayana is pivotal in heightening the stakes of the conflict and emphasizing the themes of dharma and adharma. His exploits showcase the might of Ravana's forces and underscore the challenges faced by Rama and his allies.

Indrajit's battles serve as key moments in the narrative, illustrating the power of divine intervention and the triumph of righteousness. His death at the hands of Lakshmana is a testament to the inevitability of dharma prevailing over adharma, regardless of the strength and skill of its adherents.

Indrajit's Legacy

Indrajit's legacy in the Ramayana is both awe-inspiring and cautionary. He is remembered as one of the greatest warriors in Hindu mythology, whose skills and achievements remain unparalleled. However, his story also serves as a reminder of the dangers of arrogance and the consequences of aligning with unrighteousness.

Indrajit's life is a study in contrasts a brilliant warrior whose loyalty and love for his family were overshadowed by his adherence to a path of adharma. His death marks not just the loss of Ravana's strongest defender but also a moral victory for the forces of dharma, paving the way for Rama's ultimate triumph.

Through his character, the Ramayana explores the complexities of morality, loyalty, and the eternal struggle between good and evil, making Indrajit a compelling figure whose story continues to resonate across generations.

7. Sampati

Sampati, the elder brother of Jatayu, was not a direct warrior but provided crucial information about Sita's location in Lanka. His knowledge turned the course of events, highlighting how information could be as powerful as weapons in a war.

8. Hanuman

While not insignificant in status, Hanuman's military contributions, especially during the battle and the search for Sita, are often eclipsed by his devotion to Rama. His strength and clever tactics, including burning Lanka and uprooting mountains, were crucial in Rama's victory.

9. Akampana

Akampana, one of Ravana's generals, advised Ravana to abduct Sita to avenge the deaths of other rakshasas. His counsel, though malicious, catalyzed the chain of events leading to the epic's climax.

10. Kumbhakarna

Kumbhakarna, Ravana's brother, is often remembered for his size and appetite. However, his loyalty and valor on the battlefield, even when he disagreed with Ravana's actions, demonstrated the complexity of dharma within familial bonds.

Chapter Seven - Sages Who Helped the Story Grow

1. Valmiki

Valmiki, composer of the Ramayana, plays a unique meta-role. His ashram became Sita's refuge after her exile, and he raised her sons, Lava and Kusha. His narration of Rama's story ensured its immortality, bridging the divine tale with human values.

2. Agastya

Agastya provided Rama with divine weapons and guidance during his exile. Known for his immense knowledge, he also contributed to the moral and spiritual dimensions of the story, reinforcing Rama's commitment to dharma.

3. Vishwamitra

Vishwamitra was instrumental in shaping Rama's early years. As his guru, he took Rama and Lakshmana on their first adventures, teaching them the use of celestial weapons and laying the foundation for their later exploits.

4. Sharabhanga

Sharabhanga, a sage living in the Dandakaranya forest, guided Rama during his exile. His ascetic life and wisdom reinforced Rama's understanding of the spiritual path, enriching the epic's philosophical depth.

5. Matanga

Matanga's ashram, where Shabari resided, served as a spiritual waypoint for Rama during his journey. Though not present in the story directly, his teachings to Shabari played a significant role in shaping her devotion, which in turn inspired Rama.

Chapter Eight - Mothers Who Suffered Most

1. Kaushalya

Kaushalya, the eldest queen of Dasharatha and the mother of Rama, epitomizes the quiet suffering of a mother torn between love for her son and loyalty to dharma. Her joy at Rama's coronation turned to despair when Kaikeyi's demands sent him into exile. Despite her heartbreak, Kaushalya did not openly oppose Dasharatha, showcasing her grace and resilience. Her maternal pain was compounded by witnessing the grief-stricken demise of her husband, but her faith in Rama's return never wavered. Kaushalya's character reflects patience and the strength of a mother who endures separation for the greater good, embodying the silent sacrifices women often make.

2. Kaikeyi

Kaikeyi, often painted as the antagonist, presents a nuanced portrayal of maternal anguish and manipulation. She was a loving mother to Bharata and a devoted wife to Dasharatha, but her insecurities and susceptibility to Manthara's influence led her to demand Rama's exile. Though her actions were driven by her desire to secure Bharata's throne, they brought her immense guilt and alienation. Kaikeyi's arc is one of deep remorse; her love for Rama was evident when she longed for his return to Ayodhya. Her story highlights the complexities of maternal instincts, power struggles, and the consequences of succumbing to fear and jealousy.

3. Sumitra

Sumitra, the second queen of Dasharatha and the mother of Lakshmana and Shatrughna, is a beacon of wisdom and quiet strength in the Ramayana. When Lakshmana chose to accompany Rama during his exile, Sumitra did not grieve but instead encouraged him to serve his elder brother faithfully. Her words, "Consider Rama as Dasharatha, and Sita as me," show her remarkable ability to place dharma above personal loss. Sumitra's unyielding support for her sons and her ability to suppress her emotions for the sake of righteousness demonstrate her as a mother who prioritizes duty and family honor over her own desires.

4. Mandodari

Mandodari, the wife of Ravana and mother of Indrajit, is one of the most tragic maternal figures in the Ramayana. A woman of great virtue and wisdom, she repeatedly advised Ravana to return Sita to avoid destruction but was ignored. Her sorrow deepened as she witnessed the deaths of her son Indrajit and her husband. As a mother, Mandodari's helplessness in preventing the catastrophic choices of her family made her grief even more poignant. Her enduring love and loyalty to Ravana, despite his flaws, and her ultimate heartbreak highlight the struggles of a mother caught in a web of pride and fate.

5. Sita

Sita, the epitome of devotion, courage, and endurance, is not only a central figure in the Ramayana but also one of the most profoundly affected mothers in the epic. Her journey as a mother is deeply intertwined with her identity as a wife and queen. After being abandoned by Rama due to societal pressures, Sita raised her twin sons, Lava and Kusha, in Valmiki's hermitage. Despite her heartbreak, she instilled in them values of dharma, bravery, and respect for their father.

Sita's trials as a mother began long before her children were born. During her time in Lanka, she endured immense suffering, staying resolute in her faith despite Ravana's constant attempts to break her spirit. Even after her rescue, the public's suspicion of her chastity led to her agnipariksha (trial by fire), which she endured with dignity. However, the ultimate betrayal came when she was banished while pregnant, a decision that left her isolated and heartbroken.

In Valmiki's hermitage, Sita displayed immense strength, focusing on raising her sons to be virtuous and brave despite her personal anguish. Lava and Kusha grew up unaware of their royal lineage, guided by Sita's teachings and Valmiki's wisdom. When the twins eventually confronted Rama during the Ashwamedha Yajna, they embodied the values Sita had instilled in them, showcasing her success as a mother despite her suffering.

Sita's ultimate sacrifice came when, after reuniting with Rama and proving her purity once again, she chose to return to Mother Earth rather than continue living in a society that doubted her integrity. Her decision was a testament to her unyielding self-respect and her unwillingness to compromise her principles for societal acceptance.

As a mother, Sita represents resilience and unconditional love. She endured unimaginable hardships yet ensured that her children grew up with the strength of character and commitment to dharma. Her story is a poignant reminder of the strength of mothers who, even in the face of adversity, prioritize their children's well-being while upholding their own values.

Sita: The Eternal Symbol of Strength, Devotion, and Sacrifice

Sita, the central female protagonist of the Ramayana, is one of the most revered figures in Indian mythology. Her story is a timeless tale of love, resilience, and motherhood. Born as the daughter of King Janaka of Mithila, Sita was found as a baby in a furrow during a plowing ceremony, symbolizing her divine origins as a daughter of Bhumi Devi (Mother Earth). Her life is an extraordinary blend of joys and trials, which she faced with unwavering faith and dignity.

Sita's Early Life and Marriage

Raised in Mithila, Sita was celebrated for her unparalleled beauty, wisdom, and strength. She married Rama, the prince of Ayodhya, after he broke the divine bow of Lord Shiva in a swayamvara. Their union symbolized an ideal partnership, rooted in love and mutual respect. Sita accompanied Rama to Ayodhya, embracing her role as a devoted wife and future queen.

When Rama was exiled to the forest for fourteen years, Sita chose to accompany him, despite the hardships that lay ahead. Her decision to leave the comforts of the palace to support her husband reflects her steadfast devotion and deep understanding of dharma.

Sita's Trials in the Forest and Lanka

In the forest, Sita displayed remarkable resilience and adaptability. Her abduction by Ravana, the king of Lanka, marked the beginning of her greatest trials. Despite being confined in the Ashoka Vatika, Sita refused to yield to Ravana's advances, demonstrating her unshakeable commitment to Rama. Her faith in dharma and her courage to stand against Ravana's power became defining aspects of her character.

Sita's steadfastness was rewarded when Rama, with the help of Hanuman and the Vanara army, defeated Ravana and rescued her. However, her trials did not end with her rescue. Rama's initial doubts about her chastity led her to undergo the agnipariksha (trial by fire), which she passed, proving her purity.

Sita's Role as a Queen and Her Exile

Returning to Ayodhya, Sita assumed her duties as queen. However, her happiness was short-lived. Rumors questioning her chastity resurfaced among the citizens of Ayodhya, compelling Rama to make a heart-wrenching decision. Despite knowing her innocence, he exiled her to uphold his duty as king and protect the honor of his kingdom.

Pregnant and abandoned, Sita found refuge in Sage Valmiki's hermitage. Her exile is one of the most poignant episodes in the Ramayana, highlighting the societal pressures that often outweigh personal relationships.

Sita as a Mother

In Valmiki's hermitage, Sita gave birth to twins, Lava and Kusha. Despite her sorrow, she devoted herself to raising her sons with strong values of dharma and righteousness. She taught them to respect their father and prepare for their future roles as warriors and leaders.

Sita's role as a mother is marked by resilience and love. She shielded her children from her own pain, ensuring they grew up with courage and compassion. Her teachings bore fruit when Lava and Kusha unknowingly confronted Rama's army during the Ashvamedha Yajna, showcasing their valor and adherence to dharma.

The Final Reunion and Sacrifice

When Lava and Kusha's lineage was revealed, Sita was reunited with Rama. However, societal doubts persisted, and Rama requested Sita to undergo another test of purity. Refusing to compromise her dignity further, Sita invoked her mother, Bhumi Devi, to take her back. In a dramatic moment, the Earth opened, and

Sita disappeared, leaving behind a legacy of strength and self-respect.

This act was not one of defeat but a powerful assertion of autonomy. Sita's final departure symbolized her rejection of injustice and her ultimate return to her divine origins.

Sita's Legacy as a Symbol of Strength and Dharma

Sita's life is a testament to the ideals of dharma, resilience, and unconditional love. As a wife, she epitomized devotion; as a queen, she upheld righteousness; and as a mother, she instilled values of courage and compassion in her children. Her ability to endure suffering with grace and her commitment to her principles has made her an enduring symbol of womanhood.

Her story transcends time, inspiring generations with its lessons on dignity, sacrifice, and self-respect. Sita's legacy is not just her trials and triumphs but also her ability to balance her roles as a wife, queen, and mother, leaving an indelible mark on the cultural and spiritual fabric of India.

Life Sketch of Urmila: The Unsung Heroine of the Ramayana

Urmila, the younger daughter of King Janaka of Mithila and Queen Sunaina, is a character of immense strength and grace in the Ramayana. Despite her relative obscurity in the epic, her life is a tale of profound sacrifice, silent endurance, and unwavering devotion.

This detailed narration explores Urmila's journey from her birth to her ultimate destiny.

1. Childhood in Mithila

Urmila was born into the royal family of Mithila, known for its commitment to dharma and wisdom. Her father, King Janaka, was a philosopher-king, and her upbringing reflected the values of compassion, intellect, and righteousness.

- **Education and Upbringing**: Like her elder sister Sita, Urmila was educated in the scriptures, arts, and warfare. She excelled in painting and was known for her keen intellect and artistic talents.

- **Sisterly Bond**: Urmila shared a deep bond with Sita, growing up as her closest confidante. They were not just sisters but also best friends, sharing dreams, secrets, and aspirations.

2. Marriage to Lakshmana

Urmila's life took a significant turn when Sita's swayamvara was announced. Rama won Sita's hand by lifting and stringing the divine bow of Shiva. Following this, Janaka proposed the marriages of his other daughters to Rama's brothers to strengthen the familial bond.

- **The Wedding**: Urmila was married to Lakshmana, the devoted younger brother of Rama. Their marriage was a union of mutual respect and understanding, though its trajectory was vastly different from Sita and Rama's relationship.

• **A Promise of Love**: Urmila, deeply in love with Lakshmana, envisioned a life of companionship and shared purpose. Little did she know that her life would soon be shaped by unparalleled sacrifices.

3. The Exile and Urmila's Greatest Sacrifice

When Kaikeyi demanded Rama's exile, Lakshmana decided to accompany his brother, leaving Urmila behind in Ayodhya. This decision marked the beginning of Urmila's silent suffering and unwavering support for her husband's duty.

• **Farewell to Lakshmana**: Urmila's farewell to Lakshmana was heart-wrenching. While deeply pained by his decision, she understood and supported his duty toward Rama and Sita. Urmila asked Lakshmana to go without worrying about her, vowing to take care of their family in his absence.

• **The Sacrifice of Sleep**: According to a popular legend, Urmila made an extraordinary sacrifice by surrendering her sleep for 14 years so that Lakshmana could remain ever vigilant in the forest. This act of selflessness and devotion highlights her silent contribution to Rama's mission.

• **Loneliness in Ayodhya**: In Lakshmana's absence, Urmila lived a life of solitude, fulfilling her duties toward the royal family and supporting Queen Kaushalya, Queen Sumitra, and Bharata during Rama's exile.

4. Life during the Exile

Urmila's role during the exile was crucial but often overlooked. She endured the separation with grace, dedicating herself to prayer and meditation.

• **Strengthening the Family**: Urmila became a pillar of support for the grieving royal household. She consoled Queen Sumitra and reassured Bharata, who was devastated by Rama's absence.

• **Inner Strength**: Despite her suffering, Urmila never expressed bitterness or resentment. Her silence became a testament to her inner strength and unwavering faith in dharma.

5. Reunion and Joy

The end of the 14-year exile brought immense joy to Urmila, as she was finally reunited with Lakshmana.

• **Lakshmana's Return**: When Lakshmana returned to Ayodhya with Rama and Sita, Urmila's patience and endurance were rewarded. Her reunion with her husband was a moment of profound joy and relief.

• **Coronation of Rama**: Urmila played a significant role during the coronation ceremonies, ensuring the smooth execution of the grand event.

6. Life after Rama's Coronation

After Rama's return, Urmila continued to play a supportive role in the royal household. She remained a devoted wife to Lakshmana and a dutiful member of the extended family.

• **Raising the Twins**: Urmila played a pivotal role in raising her sons, Angada and Chandraketu, who were born after Rama's coronation. She instilled in them the values of dharma and loyalty, much like their father.

• **Lakshmana's Departure**: Urmila faced another trial when Lakshmana chose to leave the mortal world as part of his duty to Rama. Though devastated, she accepted his decision with the same grace that had defined her life.

7. Urmila's Legacy

Urmila's life is a testament to silent strength and sacrifice. While the Ramayana primarily focuses on the valor of its male heroes and the trials of Sita, Urmila's story serves as a reminder of the unseen sacrifices made by those in the background.

• **The Unsung Heroine**: Urmila's sacrifices were no less significant than those of Sita or Lakshmana. Her endurance, patience, and unwavering support were instrumental in upholding dharma.

• **Symbol of Silent Strength**: Urmila's life embodies the virtues of resilience, selflessness, and devotion. Her legacy, though often overshadowed, is one of profound inspiration.

Urmila's journey from being a carefree princess in Mithila to a devoted wife and enduring figure in Ayodhya is a tale of extraordinary sacrifice and inner strength. Her life, marked by separation, loneliness, and silent suffering, highlights the often-unacknowledged contributions of women in upholding dharma and family values. Urmila remains a symbol of silent strength, proving that even those who work behind the scenes can leave an indelible mark on history.

Chapter Nine - Five significant and turbulent events in the Ramayana that shaped its narrative and left an everlasting impact

1. Rama's Coronation Fiasco

The Sudden Turn of Joy into Sorrow

The grand preparations for Rama's coronation as the crown prince of Ayodhya marked one of the most jubilant moments in the Ramayana. Citizens celebrated, and King Dasharatha was filled with pride as he announced that his eldest and most virtuous son would succeed him. However, this joyous occasion took a shocking turn when Queen Kaikeyi, influenced by her maid Manthara, demanded her two boons: Rama's exile and Bharata's coronation.

• **Dasharatha's Agony**: The king, devastated and powerless due to his vow, tried in vain to change Kaikeyi's mind. His heart broke as he was forced to banish his beloved son.

• **Rama's Acceptance**: Rama, ever dutiful, accepted the decision without hesitation. His composure stood in stark contrast to the turmoil around him.

• **Sorrow of Ayodhya**: The city plunged into grief as its beloved prince departed, and the coronation turned into a day of despair. The incident exemplifies the unpredictability of life and the cruel irony that often accompanies adherence to dharma.

2. Sita's Abduction by Ravana

A Terrifying Moment of Betrayal and Loss

The abduction of Sita by Ravana is one of the most harrowing episodes in the Ramayana. During their exile in Panchavati, Sita's compassion and curiosity led her to fall prey to Ravana's sinister plan. Disguised as a mendicant, Ravana exploited Sita's virtue and trust.

- **The Golden Deer Deception**: Ravana's scheme began with his ally Maricha transforming into a golden deer to lure Rama and Lakshmana away from their hermitage. Despite Rama's warnings, Sita insisted on capturing the deer, setting the trap in motion.

- **Sita's Abduction**: While Rama and Lakshmana were away, Ravana revealed his true form and forcibly abducted Sita, taking her to Lanka in his celestial chariot.

- **The Dying Jatayu**: The valiant vulture Jatayu attempted to save Sita but was gravely wounded by Ravana. His sacrifice underscored the gravity of the crime.

- **Sita's Helplessness**: Alone and captive in Lanka, Sita's plight symbolized the vulnerability of virtue in the face of adharma (unrighteousness). This event became the catalyst for the Great War that followed.

3. Rama's Exile

The Ultimate Test of Obedience and Resilience

Rama's exile to the forest for 14 years was a devastating blow, not only for him but also for his family and Ayodhya. The decision, stemming from Kaikeyi's boons, tested the principles of dharma and the bonds of familial love.

•	**Sacrifice of the Royal Life**: Rama willingly abandoned his royal comforts and accepted the harsh realities of forest life, demonstrating his unwavering commitment to duty.

•	**Sita's Decision**: Despite Rama's insistence that she stay in Ayodhya, Sita chose to accompany him, epitomizing the ideal of marital devotion.

•	**Lakshmana's Loyalty**: Lakshmana too renounced his life in the palace to serve Rama, showcasing the strength of brotherly love.

•	**Dasharatha's Death**: The grief of separation from Rama overwhelmed Dasharatha, who passed away shortly after his son's departure, fulfilling the curse of Shravan Kumar's parents.

4. Bharata's Actions during Rama's Exile:

A Brother's Rebellion against Injustice

Upon learning of Rama's exile and his unwitting coronation, Bharata, Kaikeyi's son, was horrified. He rejected his mother's schemes and undertook a perilous journey to the forest to bring Rama back to Ayodhya.

- **Bharata's Renunciation**: Despite being offered the throne, Bharata refused to rule in Rama's absence, declaring that he was unworthy of it.

- **The Meeting in Chitrakoot**: In a heart-wrenching encounter, Bharata begged Rama to return, but Rama, bound by dharma, declined.

- **Symbolic Coronation of Rama**: Bharata took Rama's sandals and placed them on the throne as a symbol of Rama's authority, vowing to rule only as his representative.

- **Austerity in Nandigram**: Bharata lived like an ascetic during Rama's exile, demonstrating unparalleled devotion and selflessness. His actions reinforced the ideal of brotherly love and loyalty.

5. Lakshmana's Decision to Join Rama in Exile

A Brother's Unwavering Devotion

Lakshmana's decision to accompany Rama and Sita into exile was a defining moment in the Ramayana. Despite being newly married to Urmila, he prioritized his duty toward his elder brother over his personal happiness.

- **Farewell to Urmila**: Lakshmana bid an emotional farewell to his wife, entrusting her to the care of the royal family. Urmila, understanding his dharma, supported his decision with grace and strength.

•   **A Life of Sacrifice**: During the exile, Lakshmana took on the role of protector, building shelters, guarding the hermitage, and ensuring the safety of Rama and Sita.

•   **The Fierce Defender**: Lakshmana's devotion was evident in his fiery responses to any threat against Rama and Sita, including his encounter with Surpanakha and his duel with Indrajit.

•   **The Lakshmana Rekha**: His act of drawing the protective line around their hermitage to safeguard Sita symbolized his deep concern and commitment, though it indirectly led to Sita's abduction.

These five turbulent events—Rama's coronation fiasco, Sita's abduction, Rama's exile, Bharata's selfless actions, and Lakshmana's sacrifice—are among the most impactful moments in the Ramayana. They highlight themes of duty, love, loyalty, and sacrifice, showcasing the complexities of human relationships and the trials that come with adhering to dharma. Each instance shaped the epic's trajectory and left profound lessons for its audience.

Chapter Ten - The Life of Bibhishan: Betrayal or Upholding Dharma?

Bibhishan, a central figure in the Ramayana, has often been a subject of debate among scholars and devotees. While some perceive him as a traitor to his homeland, others celebrate him as a righteous soul who upheld dharma in the face of adversity. His life is a fascinating blend of devotion, moral courage, and steadfast adherence to righteousness, offering valuable lessons on ethics and duty.

Early Life and Characteristics

Bibhishan was born as the youngest son of Sage Vishrava and Kaikesi, making him the brother of Ravana and Kumbhakarna. Unlike his elder siblings, Bibhishan was deeply spiritual and inclined towards dharma from an early age. His devotion to righteousness and Lord Vishnu set him apart in the otherwise asuric (demonic) family.

Despite being raised in a family that glorified power and conquest, Bibhishan maintained a pious and virtuous disposition. He devoted himself to studying the Vedas and scriptures, often meditating and seeking higher spiritual truths. His life symbolized the principle that one's environment need not dictate one's values.

Bibhishan's Role in Lanka

As a member of Ravana's court, Bibhishan held an important advisory position. He was a wise counselor and always prioritized dharma over personal gain or familial loyalty. His advice often contradicted Ravana's ambitions, which eventually strained their relationship.

When Ravana abducted Sita, Bibhishan was the only one in the court who dared to oppose this act. He urged Ravana to return Sita to Lord Rama, warning him of the dire consequences of such an adharma (unrighteous act). His words reflected not only his devotion to dharma but also his concern for the welfare of Lanka and its people.

However, his truthful counsel was met with scorn and rejection. Ravana, blinded by arrogance and his obsession with power, dismissed Bibhishan's warnings and accused him of disloyalty.

The Turning Point: Was Bibhishan a Traitor?

Bibhishan's decision to leave Lanka and join Lord Rama has often been labeled as an act of betrayal. To understand this, it is crucial to analyze his motivations and the context of his actions.

1. **Adherence to Dharma**:

Bibhishan's allegiance was not to Ravana's tyranny but to the universal principles of dharma. By opposing Ravana, he was not betraying his homeland but rather saving it from inevitable destruction.

2.   **Concern for Lanka**:

His repeated attempts to counsel Ravana were driven by his desire to protect Lanka and its people from the consequences of Ravana's actions. When his warnings were ignored, he saw no choice but to distance himself from Ravana's adharma.

3.   **Alignment with Divine Will**

Bibhishan recognized that Lord Rama was an incarnation of Lord Vishnu and saw it as his duty to assist Him in restoring dharma. His defection to Rama's side was not an act of treachery but of aligning himself with divine will and righteousness.

Bibhishan's choice to leave Lanka was an act of moral courage. He sacrificed familial bonds and endured the label of "deshdrohi" (traitor) to uphold the higher principles of truth and justice.

Contribution to the Ramayana

Bibhishan's contributions to the Ramayana are immense and multifaceted. His wisdom, loyalty to dharma, and strategic guidance played a pivotal role in Rama's victory over Ravana.

1.   **Strategic Counsel**:

Bibhishan provided critical intelligence about Lanka's fortifications, Ravana's strengths and weaknesses, and the secrets of the asura army. His insights gave Rama's army a significant advantage in the battle.

2.   **Moral Guidance**:

He served as a moral compass for Rama's army, emphasizing the importance of ethical warfare. For instance, his advice to Rama on how to defeat Ravana demonstrated his deep understanding of dharma and warfare.

3.   **Restoration of Dharma**:

After Ravana's death, Bibhishan was crowned the king of Lanka. As a ruler, he worked tirelessly to restore dharma and ensure the prosperity and happiness of his people. His reign marked a new era for Lanka, free from the shadow of Ravana's tyranny.

Misinterpretations and the Label of "Deshdrohi"

Bibhishan's decision to join Rama's camp has often been misinterpreted as an act of betrayal. Several factors contribute to this perception:

1.   **Cultural Bias**:

In certain narratives, loyalty to one's family and homeland is prioritized over adherence to universal principles. From this perspective, Bibhishan's actions are seen as disloyalty rather than moral courage.

2.   **Association with Ravana**:

Ravana is revered in many traditions for his devotion to Lord Shiva and his scholarly achievements. Bibhishan's opposition to Ravana is sometimes viewed as a rejection of these virtues, further fueling the "traitor" label.

3.   **Simplistic Narratives**:

Popular retellings of the Ramayana often simplify complex characters, reducing Bibhishan to a "turncoat" without exploring the ethical depth of his choices.

Despite these misinterpretations, Bibhishan's actions were guided by unwavering adherence to dharma, making him a hero in his own right.

Legacy and Lessons from Bibhishan's Life

Bibhishan's life offers several profound lessons:

1.   **Courage to Uphold Righteousness**:

His decision to stand against his brother and side with Rama exemplifies the courage needed to uphold truth and justice, even at great personal cost.

2.   **The Primacy of Dharma**:

Bibhishan's story underscores the importance of prioritizing dharma over familial or nationalistic loyalty. True loyalty lies in serving righteousness and the greater good.

3.   **Leadership and Governance**:

As the ruler of Lanka, Bibhishan demonstrated that ethical governance is the foundation of a prosperous and harmonious society.

4.   **Spiritual Wisdom**:

Bibhishan's life highlights the value of spiritual knowledge and devotion in navigating life's challenges and making difficult decisions.

Summary: Was Bibhishan a Betrayer?

Labeling Bibhishan as a traitor is a superficial interpretation of his life and actions. Far from betraying his homeland, he saved Lanka from destruction by aligning himself with dharma. His courage, wisdom, and unwavering devotion to righteousness make him a pivotal figure in the Ramayana and a timeless exemplar of ethical integrity.

Bibhishan's story reminds us that true loyalty lies not in blind allegiance but in upholding truth and justice, even when it demands great personal sacrifice. His life continues to inspire generations, proving that adherence to dharma is the highest duty of all.

Bibhishan's Family Life: A Tale of Devotion and Duty

Bibhishan, despite being surrounded by the asuric (demonic) influences of his family, led a life deeply rooted in dharma and righteousness. His family life reflects his spiritual values and unwavering commitment to the principles of truth and justice.

Marriage and Spouse

Bibhishan was married to **Sarama**, a noble and virtuous woman who shared his dedication to dharma. Sarama was one of the few members of the asura clan who opposed Ravana's unrighteous acts. She played a supportive role in Bibhishan's life, often acting as a mediator and observer in crucial moments during the events of the Ramayana.

Sarama's wisdom and compassion were evident when Sita was held captive in Lanka. She secretly consoled Sita in the Ashoka Vatika, assuring her of Lord Rama's eventual victory and warning her of Ravana's malicious intentions. Sarama's actions demonstrated her alignment with Bibhishan's values and her commitment to protecting dharma.

Their marriage was one of mutual respect, understanding, and shared spiritual ideals. Sarama's steadfast support strengthened Bibhishan's resolve during his difficult decisions, including leaving Lanka to join Lord Rama.

Children

Bibhishan is believed to have had at least two children, **Trijata** and a son whose name varies in different Ramayana versions.

1.   **Trijata**:

Trijata is a significant character in the Ramayana, remembered for her kindness and devotion to dharma. Like her parents, she opposed Ravana's actions and often acted as a confidante to Sita. She played a crucial role in comforting Sita during her captivity and conveyed messages of hope and reassurance about Lord Rama's impending victory.

Trijata's moral strength and empathy were remarkable, given the corrupt environment she was raised in. Her actions exemplify the power of righteousness, even in adverse circumstances.

2.   Bibhishan's Son:

Some regional versions of the Ramayana mention Bibhishan's son, though his role is less prominent. He is depicted as loyal to his father and supportive of his decision to uphold dharma.

Relationship with His Siblings

Bibhishan's family life was deeply influenced by his relationships with his siblings, Ravana and Kumbhakarna.

1.   Ravana:

As the youngest sibling, Bibhishan often tried to counsel Ravana against his impulsive and adharma-driven actions. Despite their familial bond, Ravana's arrogance and disregard for dharma led to a strained relationship. Ravana viewed Bibhishan's allegiance to dharma as a betrayal of their family, culminating in Bibhishan's exile from Lanka.

2.   Kumbhakarna:

Bibhishan shared a more cordial relationship with Kumbhakarna, who, despite his loyalty to Ravana, recognized Bibhishan's righteousness. However, Kumbhakarna's allegiance to family over dharma often put him at odds with Bibhishan's principles.

Life after the War

Following the defeat of Ravana and the Summary of the Ramayana war, Bibhishan was crowned as the king of Lanka by Lord Rama. As a ruler, he ensured that his family and kingdom were governed by the principles of dharma.

1.   **Reconciliation with Family**:

As king, Bibhishan worked to heal the rifts within his family caused by the war. He sought to unite the surviving members of his clan, including Ravana's widows and children, ensuring their well-being under his reign.

2.   **Role of Sarama and Trijata**:

Sarama and Trijata likely played key roles in Bibhishan's court, offering wisdom and support in administrative and spiritual matters. Their presence symbolized the triumph of virtue and righteousness in Lanka's royal household.

Legacy

Bibhishan's family life is a testament to the power of righteousness in overcoming adversity. Despite being born into a family that prioritized power and conquest, he and his family upheld dharma and worked toward restoring harmony in Lanka.

- **Sarama** represents the strength and wisdom of a devoted spouse.

- **Trijata** embodies compassion and the courage to stand for truth, even in hostile circumstances.

- Bibhishan's family, as a whole, became a beacon of hope for the citizens of Lanka, proving that adherence to dharma leads to lasting peace and prosperity.

In essence, Bibhishan's family life was a reflection of his spiritual values, marked by harmony, wisdom, and an unwavering commitment to dharma.

Ravana, the legendary king of Lanka from the Ramayana, is most famously associated with his principal queen, Mandodari. However, various texts and regional traditions mention several other wives of Ravana, each contributing unique aspect to his story. While the Ramayana by Valmiki does not elaborate much on these queens, later works like the Adbhuta Ramayana, Ananda Ramayana, and various folk traditions provide additional details.

Chapter Eleven - Some legendry women in Ravan's life shown in Ramayana

1. Mandodari – The Principal Queen

Mandodari, the daughter of Mayasura (the king of the asuras) and Hema (an apsara), is the most well-known wife of Ravana. She is renowned for her beauty, wisdom, and virtue. Mandodari was loyal to Ravana and frequently counseled him against his reckless actions, including the abduction of Sita. Despite her husband's flaws, she stood by him and lamented his downfall, reflecting her deep sense of duty.

Mandodari also played a pivotal role in the Ramayana as a figure of wisdom, advocating for dharma and peace. Her character symbolizes the tragedy of being bound to a powerful yet flawed husband.

2. Dhanyamalini

Dhanyamalini is often mentioned in the Ananda Ramayana and regional retellings as another queen of Ravana. She was a daughter of a noble lineage and is described as being exceedingly beautiful and intelligent. Dhanyamalini, like Mandodari, is believed to have disapproved of Ravana's decision to abduct Sita, warning him of the consequences of challenging Rama.

Though her role in the epic is minor, she represents a queen bound by her duty to her husband, despite recognizing his moral failings. Her inclusion in the story emphasizes the internal dissent within Ravana's own household regarding his actions.

3. Maya or Vajramala

In some versions of the Ramayana, Maya or Vajramala is mentioned as one of Ravana's queens. She is described as a celestial being, either a nymph or an asura princess, whom Ravana married during his conquests. Her character is less developed in mainstream texts, but some folklore portrays her as a queen who admired Ravana's power and might but did not play an active role in his court politics.

4. Sarama

Although Sarama is better known as the wife of Bibhishan, some versions of the Ramayana and regional stories depict her as a member of Ravana's harem. However, she is most prominently recognized for her role in comforting Sita during her captivity in the Ashoka Vatika. In these retellings, Sarama is portrayed as a compassionate and righteous figure, more aligned with dharma than Ravana's ambitions.

5. Other Mentioned Queens and Consorts

Ravana's conquests and dominance over various realms often resulted in alliances through marriage. While many of these queens remain unnamed in canonical texts, regional epics and folklore suggest that Ravana had several consorts, some of whom were asura or nagas (serpent beings). These alliances were political in nature, aimed at strengthening his empire rather than based on love or devotion.

Ritualistic and Symbolic Marriages

Some texts mention that Ravana performed symbolic or ritualistic marriages with celestial beings and goddesses during his ascension to power. These alliances symbolize his dominance over various realms, including the heavens. However, these relationships were often ceremonial and lacked personal depth.

Role of the Queens in Ravana's Life

1.	**Moral Opposition**:

Mandodari and Dhanyamalini consistently voiced their disapproval of Ravana's abduction of Sita. They served as his moral compass, though their advice was ultimately ignored.

2.	**Tragic Figures**:

The queens of Ravana are portrayed as tragic characters, caught between their loyalty to their husband and their recognition of his moral failings. Their inability to prevent his downfall highlights the complexities of their positions.

3.	**Symbol of Balance**:

While Ravana epitomized ambition and arrogance, his queens often represented balance and wisdom, emphasizing the internal conflict within his household and governance.

Summary

Ravana's queens, though often overshadowed by his larger-than-life persona, play significant roles in the Ramayana. Mandodari remains the most prominent, embodying wisdom and virtue, while Dhanyamalini and others represent the quieter dissent against Ravana's descent into adharma. These women, bound by duty and circumstances, reflect the nuanced dynamics of loyalty, love, and morality within the epic. Together, they highlight Ravana's complex character, serving as a counterbalance to his hubris and offering a deeper understanding of his life and legacy.

Chapter Twelve - Ravana's linage

Indrajit: The Warrior Prince of Lanka

Indrajit, also known as **Meghnada**, was the most powerful and valorous son of Ravana, the demon king of Lanka, and his principal queen, Mandodari. His life is a fascinating blend of loyalty, martial prowess, and deep devotion to his family and dharma as he perceived it. Indrajit's family life reflects his personal values and the immense pressure of living up to the legacy of Ravana while protecting Lanka.

Marriage and Wife

Indrajit was married to **Sulochana**, the daughter of the naga king Shesha. Sulochana was renowned for her beauty, wisdom, and devotion to her husband. Their marriage is often portrayed as one of love and mutual respect. Sulochana stood as a pillar of support to Indrajit, often offering him counsel during times of war and turmoil.

Sulochana's Role in Indrajit's Life

• **Support and Loyalty**: Sulochana's unwavering loyalty to Indrajit is evident throughout the Ramayana. Despite being aware of the consequences of Ravana's actions, she supported her husband in his duties as the prince of Lanka.

• **Advocate of Peace**: In some versions of the Ramayana, Sulochana is depicted as advising Indrajit to advocate for peace and reconciliation, emphasizing the futility of war against a noble adversary like Rama.

•   **Tragic Devotion**: After Indrajit's death, Sulochana's grief is a poignant moment in the Ramayana. Some versions mention her performing rites for her husband and lamenting the loss of a great warrior who died defending his family's honor.

Children of Indrajit

Indrajit's children are not prominently featured in Valmiki's Ramayana but are mentioned in some regional versions and retellings.

1.   **Son (Name Unknown)**:

Some legends mention a son of Indrajit who was too young to participate in the war. This child symbolized the continuity of Indrajit's legacy, though his story is largely unexplored.

2.   **Daughters**:
A few regional adaptations refer daughters, emphasizing Indrajit's role as a father who deeply cared for his family amidst his duties as a warrior.

Relationship with His Parents

Indrajit shared a unique bond with his parents, Ravana and Mandodari, which shaped his life and choices.

With Ravana

•   **Loyalty and Admiration**: Indrajit was fiercely loyal to Ravana and revered him as a father and a king.

He admired Ravana's strength and intelligence, often viewing his father's actions as justified, even when others questioned them.

• **Expectation and Pressure**: As Ravana's eldest son, Indrajit bore the immense responsibility of upholding the family's honor and protecting Lanka. This led him to take up arms against Rama and his allies, even when the odds were stacked against him.

With Mandodari

• **Maternal Guidance**: Mandodari's influence on Indrajit was significant. She often advised him to act with wisdom and caution, recognizing the dangers of his father's choices.

• **Emotional Anchor**: Mandodari's love for Indrajit is evident in her grief after his death. She lamented not only the loss of her son but also the futility of the war that claimed his life.

Indrajit as a Family Man

Despite his reputation as a fearsome warrior and master of illusion, Indrajit was deeply devoted to his family.

1. **Protective Husband**:

Indrajit ensured the safety of Sulochana and their household, keeping them away from the battlefield. His sense of duty extended beyond the war, reflecting his care for his wife's emotional and physical well-being.

2. **Loving Father**:

Though not elaborated in detail, Indrajit's interactions with his children (in versions where they are mentioned) portray him as a loving and caring father, ensuring they were nurtured amidst the chaos of war.

3. **Dutiful Son**:

Indrajit's loyalty to Ravana was unwavering. He took to the battlefield multiple times, even performing rituals and sacrifices to ensure his father's victory. His actions demonstrate the depth of his filial devotion.

Tragic End and Sulochana's Lament

Indrajit's death at the hands of Lakshmana is a pivotal moment in the Ramayana. Despite his immense strength and mastery of celestial weapons, Indrajit was ultimately defeated in battle.

- **Sulochana's Reaction**:

Upon hearing of Indrajit's death, Sulochana's grief is heart-wrenching. In some versions, she questions Ravana's decisions, holding him responsible for the loss of her husband. Her lament is a powerful commentary on the consequences of arrogance and the destruction of families in war.

Legacy and Mourning:

Sulochana's mourning is often portrayed as dignified and reflective of her deep love for Indrajit. She became a symbol of loyalty and strength, embodying the pain of countless families affected by war.

Indrajit's Legacy in the Ramayana

Indrajit's life is a blend of heroism, loyalty, and tragedy. His family life highlights his dual roles as a devoted husband and father and as a warrior prince committed to his father's cause.

- **A Complex Figure**: Indrajit's unwavering support for Ravana and his participation in the war reflect the complexities of familial duty versus personal ethics.

- **Sacrificial Devotion**: He is remembered for his sacrifices, both in battle and in upholding his family's honor. His death marks the turning point in the war, signifying the eventual downfall of Ravana.

Summary

Indrajit's family life paints a picture of a devoted husband, caring father, and dutiful son caught in the web of his father's ambitions. His relationship with Sulochana and his parents adds depth to his character, showcasing the human side of a warrior often remembered for his valor and magical prowess. Through his family, Indrajit's story reflects the cost of war and the enduring bonds of love and loyalty amidst the chaos.

Chapter Thirteen - Contributions of Kuber in the Ramayana

Kuber, the God of Wealth in Hindu mythology, plays a subtle yet significant role in the Ramayana. Though not directly involved in the epic's central conflict, his story is intricately tied to the origins of Ravana, the antagonist, and the setting of Lanka, which serves as the backdrop for much of the epic. Kuber's contributions to the Ramayana can be understood through his connections with Ravana, the creation of the celestial city of Lanka, and his ownership of the Pushpaka Vimana.

Kuber's Background and Relation to Ravana

Kuber, also known as Vaishravana, is the elder half-brother of Ravana. He was born to Sage Vishrava and his first wife, Ilavida, a celestial being. Kuber was a virtuous and just deity, revered for his adherence to dharma and generosity. As the eldest son of Vishrava, Kuber inherited the responsibility of preserving his family's honor and legacy.

Ravana, on the other hand, was born to Vishrava and his second wife, Kaikesi, who came from a family of Rakshasas. While Kuber and Ravana shared the same father, their differing maternal influences shaped their personalities. Kuber's adherence to righteousness stood in stark contrast to Ravana's ambition and pride. This ideological divide between the two brothers forms an essential part of the Ramayana's narrative, as Ravana's rise to power began with his usurpation of Kuber's kingdom and possessions.

Creation of Lanka

Kuber's most notable contribution to the Ramayana is his association with Lanka, the grand golden city that later became Ravana's capital. According to legend, Lanka was originally built by the celestial architect Vishwakarma for Lord Shiva. However, Ravana's ancestors, the Rakshasas, were granted dominion over the island.

Under Kuber's rule, Lanka flourished as a city of immense wealth, beauty, and prosperity. Kuber's governance reflected his virtues, and Lanka became a hub of culture, trade, and celestial activities. The golden palaces, lush gardens, and advanced infrastructure of Lanka showcased Kuber's ability to nurture and manage wealth responsibly.

The Pushpaka Vimana: A Celestial Creation

Kuber's possession of the Pushpaka Vimana, a divine flying chariot crafted by Vishwakarma, marks another significant contribution. This Vimana was a marvel of engineering, capable of traversing vast distances at the speed of thought. It was adorned with intricate designs, jewels, and gold, reflecting its celestial origin.

The Pushpaka Vimana played a crucial role in the Ramayana:

1. **Ravana's Seizure of the Vimana**: When Ravana overthrew Kuber, he not only claimed Lanka but also took possession of the Pushpaka Vimana. Ravana later used the Vimana to abduct Sita from the forest of Panchavati, an event that triggered the epic battle between Rama and Ravana.

2. **Symbol of Dharma and Adharma**: The Pushpaka Vimana serves as a metaphor for the shift in Lanka's character from Kuber's virtuous reign to Ravana's tyrannical rule. Under Kuber, the Vimana represented wealth attained through righteous means. In Ravana's hands, it symbolized the misuse of divine gift for selfish purposes.

3. **Rama's Use of the Vimana**: After Ravana's death, the Pushpaka Vimana was returned to Kuber as an act of restoring dharma. However, before that, Lord Rama used the Vimana to return to Ayodhya with Sita and Lakshmana after completing his exile. This journey, known as the Pushpaka Yatra, symbolizes the restoration of order and justice in the universe.

Kuber's Role as a Symbol of Dharma

Kuber's character in the Ramayana serves as a counterbalance to Ravana's ambition and greed. While Kuber governed with fairness and generosity, Ravana's rule was marked by arrogance and tyranny. This dichotomy highlights the Ramayana's central theme of dharma versus adharma.

Even after losing Lanka and the Pushpaka Vimana to Ravana, Kuber did not seek vengeance. Instead, he continued to fulfill his duties as the guardian of wealth, overseeing the treasures of the universe from his abode on Mount Kailasa. His resilience and ability to rise above personal loss illustrate the strength of dharma in the face of adversity.

Kuber's Legacy in the Ramayana

Though Kuber's role in the Ramayana is limited, his influence pervades the epic through the city of Lanka and the Pushpaka Vimana. His contributions serve as a reminder of the importance of righteous leadership and the responsible use of wealth and power.

Kuber's legacy is also evident in the eventual downfall of Ravana. By seizing Lanka and the Pushpaka Vimana from Kuber, Ravana disrupted the natural order of dharma, setting the stage for his eventual defeat at the hands of Lord Rama. In this way, Kuber's story serves as a prelude to the central conflict of the Ramayana, emphasizing the inevitability of justice and the triumph of virtue.

Chapter Fourteen - Comparative Analysis of Ahalya, Sita, Tara, and Mandodari

Background and Marriages

Ahalya, Sita, Tara, and Mandodari are renowned characters from Indian mythology, each having unique origins that highlight their significance in their respective narratives. Ahalya was not born in the usual way; she was created by Brahma himself as the epitome of beauty and virtue. Her creation was meant to showcase the divine perfection of womanhood. She was later married to Sage Gautama, a revered ascetic known for his wisdom and spiritual strength. Their union symbolized a balance between divine beauty and spiritual discipline.

Sita's origins are equally extraordinary. She was discovered by King Janaka while he was plowing the fields, which symbolizes her connection to the Earth (Prithvi). As the adopted daughter of King Janaka, she grew up as a princess known for her purity, grace, and intelligence. She married Lord Rama, an incarnation of Vishnu, after he successfully strung the divine bow of Shiva during her swayamvara. Sita's marriage to Rama marked her as a partner in upholding dharma and became the foundation of her legendary life.

Tara's background is celestial, as she was born to an apsara (celestial nymph). She became the queen of Kishkindha, first as the wife of Vali, the powerful monkey king, and later as the wife of Sugriva, his brother. Tara's life in the Vanara kingdom showed her as a wise and diplomatic queen, a trait that would define her role in the Ramayana.

Mandodari, the queen of Lanka, was the daughter of the demon architect Mayasura and an apsara. Despite being born in a family of asuras (demons), she embodied virtues of wisdom, loyalty, and morality. She married Ravana, the mighty king of Lanka, and became a silent yet profound figure in his court. Mandodari's life showcased the challenges of maintaining righteousness amidst chaos and arrogance.

These women, though from vastly different backgrounds, were united by their roles as wives, queens, and pivotal characters in the narratives of dharma and morality.

Major Life Challenges

Each of these women faced unique challenges that defined their lives and roles in the epic. Ahalya's life took a tragic turn when she was deceived by Indra, who disguised himself as her husband Sage Gautama. Despite her innocence, she became a victim of societal judgment and was cursed by her husband to turn into a stone. Her challenge was one of isolation, penance, and ultimate redemption, as she awaited Lord Rama's arrival to liberate her. Ahalya's story reflects the complexities of guilt, forgiveness, and divine grace.

Sita's challenges were deeply tied to her unwavering commitment to dharma. Her abduction by Ravana was a test of her faith and resilience. She remained steadfast in her devotion to Lord Rama, even in the face of Ravana's advances. Upon her return, she had to endure a trial by fire to prove her purity, highlighting societal expectations placed on women. Her ultimate departure to the Earth symbolized her rejection of injustice and her embrace of divine justice.

Tara's challenges were political and personal. She witnessed the conflict between her husband, Vali, and his brother, Sugriva, which culminated in Vali's death. Tara's wisdom and pragmatism allowed her to mediate between the warring factions, ensuring peace in Kishkindha. Despite her grief, she prioritized the kingdom's stability and guided Sugriva, showing exceptional leadership.

Mandodari's life was a tragic struggle against the arrogance of her husband, Ravana. She repeatedly warned him against abducting Sita, foreseeing the catastrophic consequences. However, her wisdom and counsel were ignored. Mandodari had to endure the destruction of her family and kingdom, making her story one of unheeded foresight and loyalty in the face of inevitable tragedy.

Virtues and Devotion

The virtues of these women are as varied as their life stories, yet they all demonstrate unwavering devotion, strength, and moral integrity. Ahalya's story is one of repentance and hope. Despite being cursed, she never lost faith in divine grace and patiently awaited her redemption. Her devotion to her husband and her ultimate liberation by Lord Rama highlight the transformative power of faith and forgiveness.

Sita is the epitome of devotion and resilience. Her loyalty to Lord Rama never wavered, even when she was separated from him and subjected to trials. She endured immense suffering with grace, embodying the ideals of dharma and self-sacrifice. Sita's unwavering commitment to righteousness and her strength in adversity make her a timeless symbol of inner strength and purity.

Tara's virtues lie in her wisdom and pragmatism. As a queen, she demonstrated exceptional leadership during times of political turmoil. Her ability to mediate conflicts and prioritize the greater good over personal grief showcased her selflessness. Tara's devotion to her family and her kingdom made her an invaluable figure in the Vanara kingdom.

Mandodari's devotion was marked by her loyalty to Ravana and her moral courage. Despite her husband's flaws, she remained steadfast in her love and duty. At the same time, she was unafraid to voice her concerns and warn him of his wrongdoings. Mandodari's wisdom and strength in enduring the downfall of her family highlight her resilience and integrity.

Symbolism and Lessons

Each of these women symbolizes profound life lessons and virtues. Ahalya's story is a testament to redemption through repentance and faith. Her transformation from a victim of deception to a symbol of divine grace teaches that forgiveness and spiritual awakening are always possible.

Sita represents the ideals of womanhood, dharma, and inner strength. Her story teaches the importance of adhering to one's principles, even in the face of immense challenges. Sita's life underscores the strength found in patience, resilience, and unwavering commitment to truth and justice.

Tara symbolizes wisdom and diplomacy. Her actions during the conflicts in Kishkindha highlight the importance of pragmatism and selflessness in leadership. Tara's story teaches that personal grief should not overshadow the greater responsibility to one's community and kingdom.

Mandodari embodies the consequences of unheeded wisdom. Her tragic life teaches the importance of listening to wise counsel and the dangers of arrogance. Despite her suffering, she remains a symbol of loyalty and moral courage, showcasing the strength required to stand firm in one's beliefs amidst chaos.

Responses to Adversity

The responses of these women to adversity reveal their resilience and moral strength. Ahalya faced isolation and societal judgment with patience and hope. Her ultimate liberation by Rama demonstrates the power of faith in overcoming hardships.

Sita responded to her trials with grace and unwavering adherence to dharma. Her resilience during her abduction and her ability to rise above societal scrutiny show her strength of character. Sita's ultimate return to the Earth symbolizes her rejection of injustice and her choice to embrace divine justice.

Tara displayed wisdom and pragmatism in the face of personal loss and political turmoil. She acted as a mediator and counselor, prioritizing peace and stability over personal grief. Tara's leadership during difficult times highlights her strength and selflessness.

Mandodari's response to adversity was marked by her moral courage and foresight. Despite her warnings being ignored, she remained loyal to Ravana and endured the destruction of her family with dignity. Her ability to maintain her integrity amidst chaos reflects her inner strength.

Summary

Ahalya, Sita, Tara, and Mandodari are timeless symbols of devotion, resilience, and moral strength. Ahalya teaches the power of repentance and forgiveness. Sita exemplifies the ideals of dharma, purity, and endurance. Tara's life highlights the importance of wisdom, pragmatism, and leadership. Mandodari's story underscores the value of foresight, loyalty, and moral courage. Together, these women offer profound lessons on navigating life's challenges with strength, compassion, and unwavering faith in righteousness. Their stories continue to inspire and guide humanity in the pursuit of virtue and justice.

Chapter Fifteen - Contributions of Vishwakarma in the Ramayana

Vishwakarma, the divine architect and engineer of the gods, plays an indispensable role in the Ramayana. His creations, both physical and celestial, form the stage for many of the epic's most significant events. From the construction of Lanka to the crafting of divine weapons and the Rama Setu, Vishwakarma's contributions showcase the divine intersection of creativity, skill, and dharma.

Creation of Lanka: A City of Gold

Vishwakarma's most notable contribution to the Ramayana is the creation of Lanka, the golden city. According to legend, Vishwakarma originally built Lanka for Lord Shiva. The city, made entirely of gold, was a masterpiece of celestial architecture, reflecting Vishwakarma's unparalleled skill.

Later, the city was entrusted to Ravana's Rakshasa ancestors and eventually came under Kuber's rule. Under Ravana, Lanka became a fortress of immense strategic importance, serving as the epicenter of the conflict in the Ramayana.

The Pushpaka Vimana: A Technological Marvel

Vishwakarma is also credited with crafting the Pushpaka Vimana, a celestial flying chariot initially gifted to Kuber. This vehicle played a pivotal role in the Ramayana:

- **Design and Functionality:**

The Vimana was a symbol of advanced engineering, capable of transporting passengers across vast distances instantly. Its luxurious interiors and divine adornments reflected Vishwakarma's artistic genius.

- **Use in the Epic:**

The Pushpaka Vimana was instrumental in several key events, including Ravana's abduction of Sita and Lord Rama's return to Ayodhya.

Weapons and Tools

Vishwakarma also crafted many divine weapons and tools used by gods and mortals in the Ramayana:

1. **Celestial Weapons:**

Vishwakarma forged many of the weapons used in the epic's battles, including the bow and arrows wielded by Lord Rama. These weapons were imbued with divine energy, ensuring their effectiveness against formidable foes like Ravana.

2. **Armor and Infrastructure:**

The fortifications of Lanka, as well as the celestial armory of the gods, were products of Vishwakarma's expertise. His creations provided both offensive and defensive capabilities, shaping the course of the war.

The Rama Setu: A Bridge to Lanka

One of Vishwakarma's most celebrated contributions to the Ramayana is the construction of the Rama Setu. Though Vishwakarma himself did not directly build the bridge, his son Nala who was a skilled engineer led the project. Nala inherited Vishwakarma's knowledge and expertise, using divine techniques to construct the bridge across the ocean.

- **Engineering Feat**:

The Rama Setu, built by Nala and the Vanara army, was a marvel of engineering, enabling Lord Rama and his forces to cross the sea and confront Ravana.

- **Symbol of Unity**:

The construction of the bridge also symbolizes unity and teamwork, as the entire Vanara army worked together under Nala's guidance to achieve the seemingly impossible.

Vishwakarma as a Symbol of Creativity and Dharma

Vishwakarma's creations in the Ramayana represent the divine intersection of creativity, dharma, and devotion. His work serves as a reminder of the potential for skill and craftsmanship to support the forces of good and uphold the cosmic order.

Legacy in the Ramayana

Vishwakarma's contributions to the Ramayana are both practical and symbolic. His creations, from the golden city of Lanka to the Rama Setu, form the stage on which the epic's drama unfolds. By enabling the triumph of dharma over adharma, Vishwakarma's work underscores the importance of divine creativity in maintaining balance in the universe.

In Summary, both Kuber and Vishwakarma enrich the Ramayana with their unique contributions. While Kuber embodies righteous governance and the responsible use of wealth, Vishwakarma's creations provide the tools and infrastructure necessary for the epic's events to unfold. Together, they highlight the interplay of human values and divine intervention in the timeless tale of the Ramayana.

Chapter Sixteen - Ahalya

Ahalya is a central figure in Indian mythology, particularly in the Ramayana, where she is celebrated as an embodiment of beauty, grace, devotion, and redemption. Her life story, marked by divine interventions, betrayal, and eventual liberation, has been interpreted as a powerful tale of human resilience and forgiveness. Here's an in-depth exploration of Ahalya's life:

1. Early Life and Creation

• Ahalya is often described as the most beautiful woman ever created. According to some texts, she was crafted by Lord Brahma himself, who shaped her from celestial elements to be the epitome of grace and beauty.

• Her name, "Ahalya," means "one without deformation" or "flawless." She represents the ideal of perfection in physical form and purity.

2. Marriage to Sage Gautama

• Ahalya was given in marriage to the sage Gautama by Brahma. Gautama was known for his wisdom, asceticism, and devotion.

• Despite the disparity in their physical appearances—Ahalya's divine beauty and Gautama's austere demeanor—their union symbolized the blending of material beauty and spiritual wisdom.

3. The Curse of Indra

•	Ahalya's most famous story revolves around her encounter with Indra, the king of the gods. Drawn by her unparalleled beauty, Indra disguised himself as Gautama to seduce her.

•	While some versions portray Ahalya as innocent and unaware of Indra's deceit, others suggest a momentary lapse in judgment on her part.

•	Sage Gautama discovered the deception and cursed both Ahalya and Indra. Indra was cursed with emasculation (later modified to be symbolic), while Ahalya was condemned to turn into a stone or live in isolation as an invisible entity, invisible to the world.

•	Gautama's curse came with a condition: Ahalya would be liberated when Lord Rama, an incarnation of Vishnu, would step on the stone or bless her.

4. Redemption by Lord Rama

•	Years later, during Lord Rama's journey with Sage Vishwamitra, he encountered Ahalya. Moved by her devotion, remorse, and unwavering patience, Rama freed her from the curse.

•	Upon liberation, Ahalya was restored to her original form, glowing with divine radiance. She reunited with Gautama and resumed her life as a devoted wife and sage.

5. Ahalya's Deeds and Teachings

Ahalya's life offers several moral and spiritual lessons:

a. Devotion and Repentance

• Ahalya's story emphasizes the power of repentance and devotion. Despite her curse, she remained steadfast in her faith, awaiting her redemption without resentment.

b. Human Flaws and Forgiveness

• Her story illustrates the susceptibility of humans to error and the possibility of redemption through divine grace. It underscores the importance of forgiveness and the ability to move past mistakes.

c. Strength and Patience

• Ahalya's silent endurance of her curse symbolizes strength and resilience. She teaches the value of patience and the ability to accept life's challenges with dignity.

d. Purity of Soul

• Despite her transgression, Ahalya's liberation highlights the idea that inner purity and genuine repentance can erase the stains of past mistakes.

6. Ahalya's Devotion

• Ahalya's devotion is highlighted in her unwavering faith in the arrival of Lord Rama. Even in her cursed state, she remained spiritually connected to the divine.

• Her liberation by Rama can be seen as a reward for her unshakable faith and spiritual discipline.

7. Symbolism in Ahalya's Story

• **Transformation and Liberation:** Ahalya's transformation from stone to a living being symbolizes spiritual awakening and liberation from ignorance or sin.

• **Divine Justice:** The story highlights the balance of justice and mercy in divine interventions, portraying Gautama's curse and Rama's forgiveness as two sides of the same moral coin.

8. Ahalya's Legacy

• Ahalya is remembered as a figure of beauty, humanity, and redemption. Her story is not just about sin and punishment but about the possibility of spiritual renewal.

• She serves as a reminder that divine grace can elevate even those who have fallen and that forgiveness is as powerful as judgment.

9. Modern Interpretations

• In contemporary readings, Ahalya's story is seen as a commentary on societal norms, the treatment of women, and the nature of justice.

• Her character resonates with themes of agency, accountability, and redemption, making her story relevant across generations.

Summary

Ahalya's life is a multifaceted tale that combines beauty, devotion, human frailty, and divine intervention. Her journey from a revered creation to a fallen woman and finally to a liberated soul offers timeless lessons about forgiveness, resilience, and the transformative power of faith.

Chapter Seventeen - The Life Sketch of Dhruva

Dhruva, one of the most revered characters in Indian mythology, is celebrated as a paragon of unwavering devotion and determination. His story, primarily found in the Vishnu Purana and the Bhagavata Purana, carries profound spiritual and moral significance. Dhruva's life exemplifies the virtues of faith, perseverance, humility, and the ultimate triumph of devotion over adversity.

Early Life and Challenges

Dhruva was born as a son of King Uttanapada and Queen Suniti. However, his father had another queen, Suruchi, who was more favored by the king. This favoritism created a rift in the family and subjected Dhruva and his mother to neglect and humiliation.

The pivotal moment in Dhruva's life came when he, as a young child, innocently tried to sit on his father's lap. Suruchi, out of jealousy, rebuked him and declared that only her son, Uttama, had the right to do so. She further mocked Dhruva, saying that if he wanted such privileges, he must seek divine blessings and be reborn as her son. Deeply hurt, Dhruva turned to his mother for comfort.

Suniti, instead of harboring resentment, encouraged Dhruva to seek solace and strength through devotion to Lord Vishnu. She advised him to pray to the Supreme Being, as only divine grace could fulfill his heart's desires and heal his wounded spirit.

Unwavering Devotion and Tapasya

Inspired by his mother's words, Dhruva, though only five years old, resolved to undertake rigorous penance to seek Lord Vishnu's blessings. With remarkable determination, he left the palace and journeyed into the forest. Guided by the sage Narada, who was moved by Dhruva's resolve, adopted strict ascetic practices.

Narada initially tried to dissuade Dhruva, citing his tender age and the hardships of penance. However, Dhruva's unshakable resolve convinced the sage of his sincerity. Narada then taught him a mantra to invoke Lord Vishnu and blessed him on his spiritual quest.

Dhruva meditated with extraordinary focus and devotion. Over time, his penance intensified to such an extent that his austerities began affecting the balance of the universe. Witnessing his unwavering devotion, Lord Vishnu appeared before Dhruva, radiant and resplendent.

Divine Blessings and Transformation

When Lord Vishnu appeared, Dhruva was overcome with awe and devotion. Unable to express himself, he stood speechless. Understanding his devotee's heart, Lord Vishnu touched Dhruva's cheek with His conch, granting him wisdom and eloquence.

Dhruva expressed his gratitude and humility, realizing that his desire for material recognition had transformed into a longing for eternal devotion to the Lord. Pleased with his sincerity, Lord Vishnu granted Dhruva a unique boon. He blessed Dhruva with an exalted position in the cosmos the Dhruva Nakshatra, or the Pole Star a symbol of steadfastness and guidance for all time.

Later Life and Legacy

Dhruva returned to his kingdom, where he was warmly welcomed. His father, King Uttanapada, repented for his earlier neglect and embraced Dhruva and Suniti. Dhruva later ascended the throne and ruled with wisdom and righteousness, earning the love and respect of his people.

His reign was marked by justice, prosperity, and devotion to dharma. Dhruva's story did not end with his kingship; his spiritual elevation as the Pole Star ensured his immortality. To this day, Dhruva Nakshatra is a guiding light in the night sky, symbolizing determination and divine grace.

Teachings and Significance

Dhruva's life offers timeless lessons:

1. **Perseverance and Determination**: Dhruva's unwavering resolve, even as a child, teaches the importance of steadfastness in pursuing goals, whether material or spiritual.

2. **Faith and Devotion**: His deep devotion to Lord Vishnu exemplifies the power of faith in overcoming obstacles and attaining higher truths.

3. **Forgiveness and Humility**: Despite the humiliation he faced, Dhruva never harbored bitterness toward his stepmother or father, showing remarkable maturity and grace.

4. **Spiritual Transformation**: Dhruva's journey from seeking material recognition to attaining spiritual enlightenment highlights the transformative power of devotion.

Summary

Dhruva's story is an eternal beacon of hope, reminding us of the power of faith, perseverance, and divine grace. His life is a testament to the fact that even the humblest beginnings can lead to the highest spiritual and moral accomplishments. As the Dhruva Nakshatra continues to illuminate the night sky, his legacy inspires countless generations to stay steadfast in their pursuit of truth and righteousness.

The connection between Dhruva and the Ramayana lies in their shared themes of unwavering devotion, divine grace, and the pursuit of righteousness, as well as subtle references in the broader spiritual and cultural context of Indian mythology. While Dhruva's story is primarily recounted in the Vishnu Purana and Bhagavata Purana, his tale resonates with the virtues embodied by Lord Rama and other characters in the Ramayana. Here's how these connections can be established:

1. Lineage and Cosmic Role

Dhruva, a descendant of the Solar Dynasty (Suryavansha), is connected to the lineage that eventually culminates in the birth of Lord Rama, the hero of the Ramayana. Dhruva's father, King Uttanapada, belongs to the dynasty founded by Svayambhuva Manu, the progenitor of mankind, and Dhruva's spiritual elevation enhances the glory of this lineage. Lord Rama, as an incarnation of Vishnu, continues the legacy of righteousness upheld by Dhruva.

Dhruva's transformation into the Pole Star (Dhruva Nakshatra) also has cosmic significance. The steady nature of the Pole Star symbolizes dharma and steadfastness, virtues central to Lord Rama's character. Both Dhruva and Lord Rama are eternal guides— Dhruva in the cosmic sense and Rama in the moral and spiritual sense.

2. Shared Themes of Devotion and Determination

Dhruva's unwavering devotion to Lord Vishnu parallels the devotion seen in several characters in the Ramayana. For instance:

• **Sita's Devotion to Rama**: Like Dhruva's unshakable focus on Lord Vishnu, Sita's faith and loyalty to Lord Rama remain steadfast despite the trials of her abduction and exile.

• **Hanuman's Devotion to Rama**: Hanuman, the epitome of devotion in the Ramayana, mirrors Dhruva's single-minded pursuit of divine grace. Both characters prioritize spiritual duty over personal comfort or gain.

• **3. Lessons of Endurance and Forgiveness**

Dhruva endures rejection and humiliation at a tender age, yet channels his pain into spiritual growth rather than resentment. Similarly, characters in the Ramayana, such as:

• **Lord Rama**: Faces exile, the loss of his wife, and betrayal without bitterness, showcasing the same resilience and forgiveness.

• **Sita**: Endures imprisonment in Ravana's palace with grace and dignity, reflecting Dhruva's ability to transform suffering into strength.

Both narratives emphasize the importance of rising above personal grievances to achieve higher spiritual and moral goals.

4. Divine Grace as a Unifying Element

In both Dhruva's story and the Ramayana, divine grace is pivotal. Dhruva attains a vision of Lord Vishnu through his devotion, while in the Ramayana:

• Lord Rama, an avatar of Vishnu, blesses and protects his devotees like Hanuman, Sugriva, and Bibhishan.

• The devotion of the characters leads to divine intervention, as seen in Sita's rescue and the ultimate victory of good over evil.

Dhruva's encounter with Lord Vishnu also foreshadows the compassionate and protective nature of Lord Rama in his interactions with his devotees.

5. Moral and Spiritual Parallels

Dhruva's story emphasizes the transformative power of faith and determination, values that are also central to the Ramayana. Both narratives:

• Highlight the importance of **dharma** (righteousness). Dhruva upholds his duties as a devotee, king, and spiritual seeker, much like Lord Rama, who prioritizes dharma above personal desires.

• Stress the triumph of devotion and righteousness over adversity, teaching that those who remain steadfast in their faith will ultimately find divine support and success.

Summary

Dhruva's life and the Ramayana are deeply connected through their shared spiritual ethos and moral teachings. Dhruva's steadfastness and devotion set a cosmic example that finds reflection in the lives of Lord Rama and his devotees. Both Dhruva and the characters of the Ramayana demonstrate that unwavering faith in the divine and adherence to righteousness can overcome any challenge, making their stories timeless sources of inspiration.

Chapter Eighteen -Significant depatures

1. Rama's Departure

Rama, the eldest and most prominent son of King Dasharatha, led a life that exemplified dharma (righteousness), courage, and compassion. His entire journey, from his birth to his ascension as the king of Ayodhya, was intertwined with the principles of duty, sacrifice, and moral righteousness.

Life and Reign:

Rama spent 14 years in exile, fulfilling the promise made by his father, King Dasharatha, to his stepmother Kaikeyi. During this period, he faced numerous challenges, including the abduction of his wife, Sita, by Ravana, which led to a monumental war in Lanka. After defeating Ravana and rescuing Sita, Rama returned to Ayodhya to claim his rightful place as king.

Rama ruled Ayodhya for many years after his return, performing his duties as a ruler with wisdom and justice. His reign is often referred to as "Rama Rajya," symbolizing an ideal society governed by fairness, virtue, and peace.

Departure from Earth:

The Uttarakanda of the Ramayana describes Rama's departure from the mortal world in a divine manner. It is said that towards the end of his reign, Rama felt the time had come for him to leave his earthly existence and return to his divine form. He chose to retire to the banks of the Sarayu River, a sacred river that is believed to be the gateway to the divine realms.

Rama entered the Sarayu River and, as he waded into the water, his divine form was revealed. In a transcendental moment, he ascended to the heavens, leaving his mortal body behind. This event marked the end of Rama's earthly incarnation and his return to his true form as Lord Vishnu. His departure signifies the completion of his divine mission on earth: to restore dharma and eliminate adharma (unrighteousness).

2. Lakshmana's Departure

Lakshmana, the second brother of Rama, is depicted as his most loyal and devoted companion throughout the Ramayana. Lakshmana's life was marked by selfless service to his brother, always prioritizing Rama's well-being and standing by his side, especially during his exile in the forest.

Role in the Ramayana:

Lakshmana accompanied Rama and Sita into exile and played a crucial role in various episodes, including the killing of Ravana's demon allies and the rescue of Sita from the clutches of the demoness Surpanakha. He was the one who drove the chariot in the battle against Ravana's army, and he was also a key figure in the battle itself. His unwavering devotion to Rama remained a hallmark of his character throughout the epic.

During the war in Lanka, Lakshmana was gravely wounded by Ravana's son, Indrajit. He fell unconscious for a time, and it was only when Hanuman brought the Sanjeevani herb that Lakshmana was revived. His life was filled with hardships and sacrifices, but his loyalty never wavered.

Departure from Earth:

After the defeat of Ravana and Rama's return to Ayodhya, Lakshmana continued to serve his brother faithfully. However, when Rama decided it was time to leave the earthly realm and ascend to heaven, Lakshmana too knew his time had come. In the Uttarakanda, it is said that after Rama's departure, Lakshmana, along with his other brothers, also entered the Sarayu River.

Like Rama, Lakshmana's divine form was revealed, and he ascended to the heavens in the same manner. The Ramayana portrays his departure as the culmination of his loyalty and service to his brother. Lakshmana's life and death represent the ideal of devotion and selflessness, and his ascension to the divine realms highlights his spiritual purity and divine connection.

3. Bharata's Departure

Bharata, the second son of King Dasharatha, is a character who stands out for his deep love and loyalty toward his elder brother Rama. Bharata's character is defined by his selflessness and his unwavering commitment to dharma. After Rama's exile, Bharata was devastated and refused to accept the throne that had been unjustly given to him by his mother, Kaikeyi. Instead, he placed Rama's sandals on the throne and ruled as a regent, waiting for Rama's return.

Role in the Ramayana:

Bharata's actions during Rama's exile reflect his deep sense of duty and righteousness. He did not want to enjoy the privileges of the kingdom while his brother was in exile. His devotion to Rama, even to the point of living a life of austerity and renunciation, portrays him as a model of selflessness and dharma.

Upon Rama's return from exile, Bharata joyfully handed over the throne to him and served him with great devotion. Bharata's life was a series of selfless acts of loyalty, putting the welfare of his family and kingdom above his own personal desires.

Departure from Earth:

After Rama's departure from the world, Bharata's life began to follow a similar path. It is said that Bharata chose to renounce his kingdom and embrace a life of asceticism. He lived out his final days in peace, meditating and focusing on his spiritual growth. When it was time for him to leave the mortal world, Bharata, like his brothers, entered the Sarayu River and ascended to heaven in his divine form.

Some versions of the Ramayana suggest that Bharata lived for a long time after Rama's departure, but eventually, he too returned to the divine realm, fulfilling his role as a dutiful son and brother. His death, like his life, was an act of renunciation, showing that true dharma often involves giving up worldly pleasures in the pursuit of higher spiritual goals.

4. Shatrughna's Departure

Shatrughna, the youngest of King Dasharatha's sons, is often overshadowed by the more prominent figures of Rama, Lakshmana, and Bharata. Despite this, Shatrughna played an important role in the Ramayana. He was fiercely loyal to his brothers, especially Rama, and was known for his bravery and skill in battle.

Role in the Ramayana:

Shatrughna's role becomes more significant during the battle against Ravana. Although he did not participate as actively as Rama and Lakshmana, he was an important figure in the defeat of Ravana's forces. He was chief of maintenance of Rama's armory during the battle. Later, Shatrughna was instrumental in the destruction of the demon Lavanasura, who had established a reign of terror in the region of Mathura. He was rewarded with the kingdom of Mathura after the demon's defeat.

Departure from Earth:

Shatrughna, unlike his brothers, does not have a particularly dramatic death in the Ramayana. After Rama's return and coronation, Shatrughna continued to serve his brothers and his kingdom. However, after a long and prosperous life, he eventually retired from the worldly affairs and sought spiritual enlightenment. In some versions of the Ramayana, it is said that Shatrughna entered the Sarayu River along with his brothers, where his divine form was revealed, and he ascended to heaven.

Shatrughna's life and death are marked by his dedication to his family and his kingdom. His ascension to the divine realm symbolizes his fulfillment of dharma and his eventual return to the divine source from which all beings originate.

Summary of Their Departures

The deaths of Dasharatha's sons, Rama, Lakshmana, Bharata, and Shatrughna, are not typical mortal deaths, but rather a transcendence of their earthly existence. Each of them ascends to the heavens in a divine manner, symbolizing their pure, virtuous lives and their ultimate return to the divine realm. Their departures from this world are marked by their deep devotion to dharma, loyalty to their family, and the fulfillment of their duties on earth. The manner in which they leave signifies the spiritual elevation of these characters, whose lives were embodiments of ideal human conduct.

In Summary, the deaths of King Dasharatha's sons underscore the Ramayana's philosophical teachings on dharma, selflessness, loyalty, and the ultimate return to the divine source after fulfilling one's purpose on earth.

Chapter Nineteen - All about Sage Narada

Sage Narada is one of the most revered and significant characters in Indian mythology, playing an important role in many Hindu texts, including the Ramayana. Narada is portrayed as a celestial sage, a divine messenger, and a counselor who possesses profound knowledge and wisdom. In the Ramayana, his contributions are essential in shaping key events and providing guidance to both gods and mortals. Narada's role can be understood through several distinct episodes where his influence is felt, his wisdom imparted, and his actions lead to significant developments in the epic.

1. Introduction to Ramayana and the Story of King Dasharatha's Sons

One of the earliest contributions of Sage Narada in the Ramayana occurs when King Dasharatha of Ayodhya has no sons, and he is deeply troubled by the absence of an heir. Narada, aware of the situation, appears at the royal court and assures the king that he will have sons through the divine blessings of the gods. Narada tells Dasharatha of a yagna (sacred fire ritual) that can be performed to receive divine boons.

Narada advises Dasharatha to perform the Putrakameshti Yagna, a ritual that will bless him with progeny. The king follows Narada's advice, and as a result, his queens; Kaushalya, Kaikeyi, and Sumitra are blessed with sons. This leads to the birth of Rama, Bharata, Lakshmana, and Shatrughna, each of whom plays a pivotal role in the Ramayana. Narada's intervention thus marks the beginning of the royal lineage that will shape the future of the epic.

2. The Birth of Rama and the Prophecy of Rama's Exile

Narada also plays a crucial role in the events surrounding the birth of Rama and the prophecy concerning his future. When Rama is born to Kaushalya, the birth is celebrated in the kingdom. Narada, through his divine insight, is aware of the cosmic importance of Rama. He knows that Rama is no ordinary human but an incarnation of Lord Vishnu, comes to earth to defeat the demon king Ravana and restore righteousness.

At one point, when the gods convene to discuss Ravana's tyranny and the need for Rama's intervention, Narada's wisdom and understanding of divine plans are instrumental in revealing the need for Rama to perform his mission on earth. Narada's role in this part of the story highlights his knowledge of the broader cosmic framework in which the events of the Ramayana unfold.

3. The Exile of Rama and the Events Leading to It

Narada's role becomes even more significant when he helps explain the divine reasons behind the exile of Rama. King Dasharatha, in a moment of weakness and in response to a demand from his wife Kaikeyi, unwittingly exiles his son Rama to the forest for 14 years. Narada is aware of the cosmic necessity of Rama's exile and reassures the gods and sages that this part of the divine plan will lead to the eventual defeat of Ravana.

While Narada doesn't directly intervene in the exile, he offers philosophical insights into the unfolding events. He subtly encourages Dasharatha to maintain his sense of dharma, knowing that this tragedy is part of a divine mission. His role as a divine messenger, who understands the larger picture, helps the characters in the epic (and readers) understand that the trials faced by Rama and his family are meant to restore cosmic balance.

4. Narada's Role in Advising Sita

During the time of Sita's abduction by Ravana, Sage Narada plays an important role in guiding both Rama and Sita. While in exile, when Rama and Sita are separated by Ravana's forces, Sita is captured by Ravana and taken to Lanka. While Rama searches for her in the forest, it is Narada who consoles and advises Sita in her difficult time.

Narada also appears before Ravana in Lanka and advises him about the consequences of abducting Sita. Although Ravana does not heed Narada's words, Narada's wisdom and moral teachings resonate throughout the epic. His counsel often highlights the importance of righteousness and divine order, serving as a guiding voice for both good and evil characters.

5. Narada's Role in the Battle between Rama and Ravana

Narada's contributions continue even during the climactic battle between Rama and Ravana. As the battle between the forces of Rama and Ravana intensifies, Narada provides guidance to the gods and celestial beings who are concerned with the outcome. Narada's role here is to help clarify the divine plan that Rama's victory is inevitable, as he is the incarnation of Vishnu, destined to destroy Ravana and restore dharma.

Narada's wisdom also assists in explaining the deeper significance of the battle. While Rama's victory is a triumph of good over evil, it is also symbolic of the restoration of cosmic order and the ultimate purpose of the divine incarnation of Vishnu on earth.

6. Narada's Role in Promoting Dharma

Throughout the Ramayana, Sage Narada stands as a symbol of wisdom and dharma. He frequently engages in discussions about the nature of dharma (righteousness) and its importance in sustaining the universe. His teachings often emphasize the importance of truth, devotion to duty, and the necessity of selfless action.

In many instances, Narada imparts his wisdom to various characters, including sages, kings, and gods. His messages are not just confined to the Ramayana, but reflect broader spiritual and ethical principles that are central to Hindu philosophy. Narada's teachings underscore the importance of aligning one's actions with divine will, regardless of personal desires or ego.

7. Narada's Relationship with the Gods and His Role as a Messenger

Narada's role as a celestial sage and messenger is another defining aspect of his character in the Ramayana. As a frequent intermediary between the gods and humans, Narada has access to divine knowledge and is tasked with delivering messages to mortals. He often brings news of events in heaven to the people on earth and vice versa.

In the Ramayana, Narada also acts as a confidant to the gods, particularly when they are concerned about Ravana's growing power. It is through Narada's advice that the gods understand the necessity of Rama's incarnation on earth and the role he will play in ending Ravana's reign.

8. Narada's Role in the Restoration of Sita's Honor

Towards the end of the Ramayana, when doubts are raised about Sita's purity after her abduction, it is Narada who plays a subtle role in reinforcing the importance of trust, truth, and righteousness. He supports the decision made by Rama to put Sita through the trial of fire (Agni Pariksha) to prove her chastity. While this episode remains controversial in later interpretations, Narada's guidance represents the understanding of dharma as it was perceived in the context of the epic.

Summary

In the Ramayana, Sage Narada's contributions are manifold, spanning from the early moments of Rama's birth to the final moments of the epic. He acts as a divine sage, advisor, and mediator, imparting profound wisdom to both gods and mortals. His interventions and guidance, whether direct or indirect, help shape the course of events and ensure the fulfillment of the divine plan. Narada's role exemplifies the ideal of spiritual wisdom, illustrating that every event, no matter how tragic, plays a part in the greater cosmic order. His character in the Ramayana is a reminder of the importance of dharma, the divine will, and the inevitability of the cosmic balance.

Chapter Twenty - Hierarchical explanation of Muni, Rishi, Acharya, Rajarshi, Maharshi, and Saptarishi depicted in Indian mythology including Ramayana

In Hindu tradition, various titles such as Rishi, Muni, Acharya, Maharishi, and others are used to denote different levels of spiritual attainment, wisdom, and renunciation. These titles reflect the individual's role in society and their spiritual journey. Here's a detailed exploration of each title, the notable figures associated with them, and the reasons behind these distinctions:

1. Rishi

• **Meaning**: The term Rishi refers to a sage or a seer, one who has attained profound spiritual knowledge, often through meditation and divine revelation. Rishis are considered to have direct access to cosmic truths and wisdom, often receiving the Vedic hymns and spiritual teachings from the gods themselves. They were instrumental in composing the Vedic texts and preserving ancient knowledge.

• **Why They Are Called Rishis**: Rishis are believed to have transcended human limitations and attained a state of divine insight. The word "Rishi" comes from the root rish meaning "to flow" or "to move," symbolizing the flow of divine knowledge that they imparted.

• **Examples and Why They Are Called Rishis**:

○ **Vishwamitra**: Vishwamitra was originally a king who, after intense penance, ascended to the status of a Rishi. He is considered a Rishi because he received divine wisdom, which led him to compose important hymns in the Rigveda.

○ **Valmiki**: Known as the "Adikavi" (first poet), Valmiki is credited with writing the Ramayana. He is regarded as a Rishi for his spiritual depth and his transformation from a hunter to a sage, who was blessed with divine knowledge to narrate the story of Lord Rama.

○ **Vyasa**: Vyasa, also called Vedavyasa, is the compiler of the Vedas and the author of the Mahabharata. He is one of the greatest Rishis for his monumental contributions to preserving spiritual knowledge and writing the epic texts.

2. Muni

• **Meaning**: A Muni is a sage or ascetic who practices austerities and meditation in order to attain self-realization. Unlike Rishis, who often receive divine revelations, Munis focus on inner enlightenment and spiritual progress through self-discipline and deep meditation.

• **Why They Are Called Munis**: The word Muni is derived from the Sanskrit root mun, meaning "to silence" or "to control the mind." Munis are thus those who silence their minds through disciplined meditation and inner exploration.

• **Examples and Why They Are Called Munis**:

o **Ashtavakra**: Ashtavakra was a sage who composed the Ashtavakra Gita, which focuses on the path of self-realization and the liberation of the soul. He is called a Muni because of his spiritual wisdom and his focus on personal meditation rather than divine revelation.

o **Kapila**: Kapila, a sage associated with the Samkhya philosophy, is also considered a Muni. His teachings focused on the duality between matter and spirit and the way to attain liberation through self-realization, making him a prominent Muni in Hindu philosophy.

3. Acharya

• **Meaning**: An Acharya is a teacher or spiritual guide who imparts knowledge of scriptures, philosophy, rituals, and spiritual practices. An Acharya is typically someone highly learned and capable of transmitting wisdom to others. While not necessarily practitioners of intense austerities like Rishis or Munis, an Acharya is a respected scholar and guru.

• **Why They Are Called Acharya**: The word Acharya comes from achara, meaning "practice" or "conduct." An Acharya is one who not only teaches knowledge but also exemplifies the principles of dharma (righteousness) through his actions and lifestyle.

- **Examples and Why They Are Called Acharya:**

○ **Adi Shankaracharya**: A philosopher and theologian, Adi Shankaracharya is considered one of the most important Acharyas. He is credited with consolidating the doctrine of Advaita Vedanta and establishing monastic orders (mathas) across India. He is called an Acharya due to his deep knowledge of the Vedas and his role in disseminating this wisdom.

○ **Ramanuja**: Ramanuja was a great philosopher who promoted the Vishishtadvaita (qualified non-dualism) school of Vedanta. He is called an Acharya because he was a teacher who guided people toward understanding the nature of the soul and the Supreme Being through his writings and teachings.

4. Maharishi

- **Meaning**: Maharishi means "Great Sage" and refers to a highly revered and enlightened Rishi. A Maharishi is a person who has attained extraordinary spiritual wisdom, often through intense meditation, austerity, and self-realization. The title signifies exceptional knowledge of the divine and the ability to guide others to the highest levels of spiritual enlightenment.

• **Why They Are Called Maharishis**: The prefix Maha means "great," and when combined with Rishi, it denotes someone who is not only a sage but also an extraordinary one. Maharishis are considered to be at the pinnacle of spiritual and intellectual wisdom.

• **Examples and Why They Are Called Maharishis**:

o **Vishwamitra**: Initially a king, Vishwamitra became a Maharishi after years of penance, meditation, and gaining spiritual power. He is called a Maharishi because of his immense wisdom and role in the spiritual and moral development of humanity.

o **Atri**: One of the Saptarishis, Atri is a Maharishi due to his profound spiritual insight and contributions to Vedic knowledge. He is revered as one of the greatest sages in Hindu tradition.

5. Rajarshi

• **Meaning**: A Rajarshi is a king who has achieved the status of a sage due to his wisdom, righteousness, and devotion to spiritual practice. These are royal figures who combine their worldly duties with a deep commitment to dharma (righteousness) and spiritual discipline.

• **Why They Are Called Rajarshi**: The term Rajarshi is a combination of Raja (king) and Rishi (sage), meaning "a king who is also a sage." Rajarshis are respected for their ability to govern with wisdom while maintaining a life of virtue and spiritual practice.

• **Examples and Why They Are Called Rajarshis**:

○ **King Janaka**: King Janaka, the father of Sita in the Ramayana, is considered a Rajarshi because of his great wisdom and spiritual insight, despite being a powerful ruler. He is known for his detachment from material wealth and his deep spiritual knowledge.

○ **King Shibi**: King Shibi is revered as a Rajarshi for his commitment to justice and dharma. He once sacrificed his own flesh to protect a dove from a hawk, exemplifying his selflessness and devotion to righteousness.

6. Saptarishi

• **Meaning**: The Saptarishi refers to the seven great sages who are considered to possess the highest level of wisdom and are believed to be eternal guides for humanity. These seven Rishis are often associated with the seven stars of the Big Dipper constellation in the sky.

• **Why They Are Called Saptarishis**: The word Saptarishi means "seven sages" in Sanskrit. These sages are believed to embody divine wisdom and serve as the guiding spirits of the universe.

• **Examples and Why They Are Called Saptarishis**:

○ **Brahmarishi Atri, Vashistha, Kashyapa, etc.**: These seven sages are highly revered and are considered the eternal spiritual leaders who guide the moral and spiritual progression of humanity. They are called Saptarishis because of their supreme wisdom and their role in maintaining cosmic order.

Summary

The titles of Rishi, Muni, Acharya, Maharishi, and others represent different levels of spiritual and intellectual accomplishment in Hindu tradition. Each of these terms reflects the individual's contributions to spiritual wisdom, their relationship with divine knowledge, and their role in guiding humanity. From the divine revelations of Rishis to the scholarly wisdom of Acharya and the spiritual greatness of Maharishis, these sages played a pivotal role in shaping the philosophical, religious, and moral foundations of Indian culture. Understanding these titles and their significance is crucial for the upcoming generation to recognize the value of wisdom, spirituality, and righteous living.

The **Saptarishi** (Seven Sages) are highly revered figures in Hindu mythology and are considered to be eternal, guiding the moral and spiritual development of humanity. They are often associated with the seven stars in the constellation of the Big Dipper, known as the Sapta Rishi Mandala in Sanskrit.

The **Saptarishis** (Seven Sages) are revered as some of the greatest spiritual beings in Hinduism, and their greatness stems from their deep wisdom, unwavering commitment to righteousness, and profound contributions to both spiritual and societal well-being. These sages are seen as guiding figures that have shaped the moral and spiritual fabric of society, offering teachings that transcend time and inspire future generations. Here's a detailed look into why the Saptarishis are so great, their contributions to society, their teachings, and their disciples.

1. Brahmarishi Atri

• **Greatness**: Atri is considered one of the oldest and most revered of the Saptarishis. His greatness lies in his wisdom, asceticism, and contributions to the Vedic knowledge. He is also revered for his devotion to Brahma and is known for his spiritual purity and deep meditation.

• **Contributions**: Atri's contributions include many hymns in the Rigveda. He also plays an important role in the cosmic creation, where he is believed to have been one of the sages who helped shape the world. Atri is credited with the discovery of the knowledge of the Atman (soul) and the understanding of the Supreme Being.

• **Teachings**: Atri emphasized the path of meditation and self-purification to achieve unity with the divine. He taught that by overcoming personal desires and focusing on the inner self, one could attain liberation.

• **Disciples**: Atri's disciples include his sons, **Durvasa**, who is famous for his temper but also for his immense spiritual power, and **Chandra**, the moon god, who was born to Atri and his wife Anasuya.

2. Brahmarishi Vashistha

- **Greatness**: Vashistha is known for his unparalleled wisdom, virtuous nature, and deep spiritual insight. He is often portrayed as the teacher of the gods, particularly his role in the Ramayana, where he instructs Lord Rama. His greatness comes from his ability to balance the path of knowledge and devotion, being a symbol of idealism and spiritual achievement.

- **Contributions**: Vashistha contributed to the Rigveda and authored texts like the Vashistha Samhita, which contains teachings on philosophy, meditation, law, and ethics. He is also known for guiding the kings and noble rulers of the time, teaching them how to rule righteously.

- **Teachings**: Vashistha emphasized the concept of self-realization and dharma (righteous duty). He taught that wisdom, meditation, and self-discipline lead to liberation, and he demonstrated the importance of practicing non-attachment and renunciation in one's life.

- **Disciples**: Vashistha had several disciples, including **Rama**, to whom he provided guidance during the latter's exile, and **Shakti**, who is also a revered sage in his own right.

3. Brahmarishi Vishwamitra

- **Greatness**: Vishwamitra's greatness lies in his incredible journey from being a king to becoming a Brahmarishi through intense penance and meditation. His quest for spiritual excellence, despite numerous challenges, makes him a symbol of perseverance and transformation.

- **Contributions**: Vishwamitra is credited with composing many hymns of the Rigveda, including the famous Gayatri Mantra. He is also the teacher of **Lord Rama**, guiding him through his various trials and tests.

- **Teachings**: Vishwamitra's teachings revolve around the pursuit of higher knowledge, meditation, and the importance of righteousness. He stressed the idea that anyone, regardless of their birth, could achieve spiritual greatness through discipline and dedication.

- **Disciples**: Vishwamitra's most prominent disciple is **Lord Rama**, whom he mentored in various aspects of life and dharma, guiding him during the difficult events of the Ramayana.

4. Brahmarishi Gautama

- **Greatness**: Gautama's greatness is rooted in his deep philosophical contributions and his ability to lead an ideal, disciplined life. He was a sage of great renunciation and lived in harmony with nature and the divine.

- **Contributions**: Gautama contributed to Vedic knowledge and is credited with establishing moral and ethical conduct for society. He was also the author of several hymns in the Rigveda. His ashram was a hub of learning and spiritual practice.

• **Teachings**: Gautama emphasized truthfulness, humility, and devotion to God. He taught that an individual must always live in accordance with dharma, making truth and righteousness central to one's life.

• **Disciples**: Gautama had several disciples, most notably his wife **Ahalya**, who is famous for her role in the Ramayana. She is a symbol of repentance and redemption, illustrating that even those who stray from the path of righteousness can return through devotion and penance.

5. Brahmarishi Jamadagni

• **Greatness**: Jamadagni's greatness lies in his strong discipline, ascetic practices, and his role as the father of **Parashurama**, one of the ten avatars of Vishnu. His life was dedicated to meditation, truth, and the welfare of society.

• **Contributions**: Jamadagni contributed to Vedic wisdom and the practice of yajnas (sacrificial rites). His teachings focused on the importance of knowledge, humility, and service to society.

• **Teachings**: Jamadagni's teachings revolved around the importance of selfless service, knowledge, and renunciation. He stressed the importance of fulfilling one's duties (dharma) and living a life of righteousness.

• **Disciples**: Jamadagni's disciple was **Parashurama**, who became one of the most renowned sages and warriors in Hindu mythology.

Parashurama's role in protecting the world from corrupt rulers was deeply influenced by his father's teachings.

6. Brahmarishi Kashyapa

• **Greatness**: Kashyapa is considered one of the most important sages in Hindu tradition. His greatness stems from his role in the creation and the propagation of life. He is revered as the father of many important figures, including the gods, demons, and sages.

• **Contributions**: Kashyapa is credited with establishing various dynasties and lineages, including those of the Devas (gods), Asuras (demons), and Rakshasas (monsters). His contributions to cosmology and creation are central to Hindu cosmology.

• **Teachings**: Kashyapa taught the importance of balance and harmony in nature. He believed that all living beings are interconnected and that humanity must live in balance with the universe.

• **Disciples**: Kashyapa's disciples include **Garuda**, the divine eagle, and **Vasuki**, the serpent king, both of whom played important roles in Hindu mythology.

7. Brahmarishi Bharadwaj

• **Greatness**: Bharadwaj is known for his profound spiritual insight and his contributions to the Vedas. His greatness is rooted in his wisdom, discipline, and his emphasis on the study of sacred texts and philosophical principles.

- **Contributions**: Bharadwaj is credited with composing parts of the Yajurveda and is also considered the founder of the Bharadwaj gotra. He is a symbol of a sage who perfectly blends knowledge and action.

- **Teachings**: Bharadwaja's teachings emphasized the importance of studying the Vedas, practicing meditation, and living a life of disciplined action. He advocated for a life led by wisdom and understanding.

- **Disciples**: Bharadwaj had several disciples, including **Drona**, who was a revered teacher and martial arts guru in the Mahabharata, responsible for training the Kauravas and Pandavas in warfare.

Summary

The Saptarishis' contributions to society and their teachings were foundational in shaping the spiritual, ethical, and societal order. Their disciples, ranging from kings to gods, continue to inspire millions. The Saptarishis taught that **through perseverance, self-discipline, wisdom, devotion, and righteousness**, one can attain spiritual elevation and influence the world for the better. Their lives and teachings remain relevant across generations, offering timeless guidance in our pursuit of truth and self-realization.

Chapter Twenty One - The Ashwamedha Yagna: A Comprehensive Explanation

The Ashwamedha Yagna is one of the most prominent and elaborative Vedic rituals, holds significant cultural, spiritual, and political importance in ancient Indian traditions. The ceremony was primarily performed by kings seeking to assert their sovereignty, validate their power, and establish their divine right to rule. This ritual, mentioned in the Vedas, Ramayana, and Mahabharata, as well as in later Puranic texts, symbolizes a blend of worldly ambition and spiritual devotion.

Understanding the Ashwamedha Yagna

Logic and Purpose

1. **Assertion of Sovereignty**:

The Ashwamedha Yagna was performed by kings to proclaim their dominance over neighboring territories. The release of a consecrated horse symbolized the king's intent to extend his rule, challenging other rulers to either submit or engage in battle.

2. **Spiritual Significance**:

The ritual sought divine approval for the ruler's sovereignty and aimed at achieving both material prosperity and spiritual merit. It was believed that the yagna would cleanse sins, secure divine blessings, and ensure the king's place in heaven.

3.   **Desire and Ambition**:

The desire for unchallenged authority and eternal glory motivated rulers to undertake this demanding ritual. It was not merely about conquest but also about legitimizing power in the eyes of subjects and the divine.

4.   **Ego and Righteousness**:

While the ritual often reflected the king's ego and desire for supremacy, it was tempered by the spiritual elements of the yagna, which emphasized self-restraint, devotion, and responsibility. The king was reminded that his power was granted by the divine and should be used for the welfare of his people.

The Process of Ashwamedha Yagna

1.   **Preparation**:

o   The king, along with his priests, selected and consecrated a flawless horse. This horse, often white or of auspicious color, was the central symbol of the ritual.

o   The yagna required substantial resources, including gold, jewels, and provisions for large gatherings of priests, scholars, and the general public.

2.   **Release of the Horse**:

o   The consecrated horse was set free to roam across territories for a year. A royal retinue, including warriors and ministers, followed the horse to ensure its safety.

o   Any king whose land the horse entered had two choices: to submit to the sovereignty of the horse's master or to fight in defense of their independence.

3.   **Return of the Horse**:

o   If the horse returned unharmed after a year, it signified the success of the king's claim to sovereignty. The victorious king reaffirmed his authority and was deemed worthy of performing the yagna.

4.   **Sacrificial Ceremony**:

o   The horse was ritually sacrificed, signifying the king's ultimate dominion over the earth.

o   This was followed by a series of offerings, chants, and prayers conducted by learned priests.

5.   **Distribution of Wealth**:

o   At the Summary of the yagna, the king distributed gifts and wealth to priests, scholars, and the general public. This act of generosity further established his reputation as a just and magnanimous ruler.

Impact on the General Public

1.   **Legitimization of Rule**:

The yagna reassured the people of the king's divine approval, strengthening their faith in his leadership.

2.   **Economic Activity**:

The large-scale organization of the yagna generated significant economic activity, providing work for artisans, traders, and laborers.

3. **Cultural Influence**:

The ritual became a cultural spectacle, with music, recitations, and discussions contributing to the intellectual and artistic environment of the time.

4. **Unity and Loyalty**:

The yagna fostered unity among the king's subjects, as they witnessed his dedication to dharma and governance.

Prominent Ashvamedha Yagnas in History

1. Lord Rama's Ashvamedha Yagna

- **Why   Performed**:
After returning to Ayodhya and establishing his rule, Lord Rama performed the Ashvamedha Yagna to reaffirm his sovereignty and absolve himself of the sin of killing Ravana, a Brahmin.

- **Process   and   Outcome**:
The horse was released and traveled across kingdoms, with Rama's loyal forces ensuring its safety. Lava and Kusha, Rama's sons (unaware of their lineage), captured the horse, leading to a confrontation. Eventually, the familial bond was revealed, and the yagna was completed successfully.

- **Achievement**:
This yagna reinforced Rama's position as an ideal king

(maryada purushottam) and demonstrated his commitment to dharma and justice.

2. Yudhishthira's Ashvamedha Yagna

- **Why Performed**:

After the Kurukshetra War, Yudhishthira performed the Ashwamedha Yagna to consolidate the Pandavas' rule and seek spiritual redemption for the immense bloodshed during the war.

- **Process and Outcome**:

Arjuna led the retinue that accompanied the horse, defeating or negotiating with various kings. The yagna was completed with grand ceremonies attended by sages like Vyasa and Krishna.

- **Achievement**:

Yudhishthira reaffirmed his authority as the ruler of Hastinapura and achieved spiritual peace. The yagna symbolized the restoration of order and dharma after the chaos of war.

3. Emperor Samudragupta's Ashvamedha Yagna

- **Why Performed**:

The Gupta emperor Samudragupta, often referred to as the "Napoleon of India," performed the Ashvamedha Yagna to celebrate his extensive military conquests across India.

- **Process and Outcome**:

Samudragupta's horse roamed freely across vast territories, with local rulers acknowledging his supremacy. The yagna's completion marked the zenith of the Gupta Empire's power.

- **Achievement**:

The ritual legitimized Samudragupta's rule and established him as a Chakravarti (universal ruler). It also symbolized the empire's cultural and economic prosperity.

Criticism and Interpretations

The Ashvamedha Yagna, while celebrated, has been critiqued by some for its inherent elements of aggression and domination. Modern scholars interpret the ritual as:

1. **A Political Tool**:

The yagna was as much a political strategy as a spiritual exercise, enabling rulers to assert dominance over rival kingdoms.

2. **A Test of Leadership**:

The success of the ritual required not only military might but also moral and spiritual integrity, making it a holistic test of kingship.

3. **A Symbolic Sacrifice**:

While the horse's sacrifice may seem harsh by modern standards, it symbolized the king's willingness to sacrifice personal desires for the greater good.

Legacy of the Ashvamedha Yagna

The Ashvamedha Yagna remains a profound symbol of ancient Indian civilization, blending material ambition with spiritual devotion. Its emphasis on dharma, unity, and responsible leadership continues to inspire discussions about governance and morality.

While the yagna is no longer practiced, its stories endure as lessons in the complex interplay of power, spirituality, and ethics, exemplifying the timeless values of Indian culture.

Chapter Twenty Two - Swayamvara Rituals: A Detailed and Critical Explanation

Swayamvara, literally meaning "self-choice of groom" (swayam = self, vara = groom), was an ancient Indian ritual that allowed a princess or a woman of noble birth to choose her husband from a group of assembled suitors. This tradition is prominently described in Vedic and Puranic literature, the Ramayana, the Mahabharata, and other Indian scriptures. It served as a unique blend of personal autonomy and social-political alliances in ancient Indian society.

The Ritual of Swayamvara

The swayamvara was an elaborate ceremony involving various stakeholders and rituals:

1.   **Announcement:**

o   A formal declaration was made, inviting eligible kings and princes to participate. This announcement often detailed the conditions or challenges the suitors had to fulfill to win the bride's hand.

o   Sometimes, eligibility was based on lineage, valor, or accomplishments.

2. **Preparation**:

o   The royal court or a grand public arena was chosen as the venue.

o   The bride was adorned in her finest attire, symbolizing her central role in the ceremony.

3. **The Test or Challenge**:

o   A key feature of the swayamvara was the test of skill, intellect, or strength that the suitors had to perform.

o   Examples include breaking a divine bow (Sita's swayamvara) or shooting a target through reflection (Draupadi's swayamvara).

4. **Choice by the Bride**:

o   After the challenge, or in its absence, the bride chose her husband by placing a garland around his neck (varmala), signifying acceptance.

5. **Marriage Ceremony**:

o   The chosen groom and the bride were married either immediately or after further rituals.

Pros and Cons of the Swayamvara Tradition

Pros

1. **Autonomy for Women**:

o   It was one of the few instances where women had agency in choosing their life partner.

o   The bride's decision was respected, even in a patriarchal society.

2.   **Promotion of Merit**:

o   The challenges emphasized qualities like valor, intelligence, and skill, ensuring that the bride married a worthy suitor.

o   This system often avoided purely political or economic marriages by emphasizing individual capability.

3.   **Political Alliances**:

o   Swayamvaras often forged alliances between powerful kingdoms, ensuring mutual cooperation and stability.

4.   **Transparency**:

o   The public nature of the ceremony ensured fairness and prevented manipulation behind closed doors.

Cons

1.   **Focus on Physical Strength**:

o   Challenges often prioritized physical prowess over emotional compatibility or other virtues, limiting the bride's options.

2.   **Exclusion of Non-Eligible Suitors**:

o   The swayamvara was limited to royal or noble men, excluding worthy individuals from lower social strata or different professions.

3.   **Potential for Conflict**:

o   Swayamvaras often resulted in disputes, leading to wars or enmity between kingdoms.

o   Rival suitors who failed to win the bride's hand sometimes reacted violently, disrupting peace.

4.   **Symbolic Autonomy**:

o   While the bride had the "choice," it was often restricted to the pre-selected group of suitors deemed worthy by her family.

Famous Swayamvaras in Indian Scriptures

1. Sita's Swayamvara (Ramayana)

•   **Conditions**:
King Janaka set the condition that the suitor had to string and break the divine bow of Lord Shiva (Pinaka). Only someone of immense strength and divine favor could accomplish this feat.

•   **Stakeholders**:

o   **Sita**: The bride.

o   **Rama**: The victorious suitor who successfully broke the bow.

o   **Other Kings and Princes**: Numerous suitors, including Ravana, who failed.

o   **Janaka and Dasharatha**: Fathers of the bride and groom, respectively.

•   **Outcome**:

o   Rama won Sita's hand, establishing a bond between Ayodhya and Mithila.

o   Ravana's humiliation planted seeds of enmity, which culminated in the events of the Ramayana.

- **Impact**:

o   While the swayamvara emphasized Rama's divine strength and Sita's fortune, it also led to Ravana's eventual obsession with Sita, resulting in her abduction and the epic battle.

2. Draupadi's Swayamvara (Mahabharata)

- **Conditions**:

The suitor had to string a massive bow and shoot an arrow targeting at an eye of a rotating fish by looking at its reflection in a pool of water below.

- **Stakeholders**:

o   **Draupadi**: The bride.

o   **Arjuna**: The successful suitor, disguised as a Brahmin.

o   **Karna**: A contender who was disqualified due to his caste.

o   **Other Kings**: Duryodhana, Shishupala, and others who failed.

o   **Drupada**: Draupadi's father, who orchestrated the swayamvara.

- **Outcome**:

o   Arjuna won Draupadi, but through a twist of fate, she became the wife of all five Pandavas.

o   The event deepened the rivalry between the Pandavas and Kauravas, contributing to the eventual war.

- **Impact**:

o   Draupadi's swayamvara was symbolic of merit and fairness but also exposed the rigid caste system's flaws and sowed discord among the Kshatriyas.

3. Amba's Swayamvara (Mahabharata)

- **Conditions**:

Amba, along with her sisters Ambika and Ambalika, was to choose her husband from the assembled suitors.

- **Stakeholders**:

o   **Amba**: The bride who loved King Shalva.

o   **Bhishma**: Interrupted the swayamvara, abducting all three princesses for his brother Vichitravirya.

o   **Shalva**: Amba's lover, who refused to marry her after her abduction.

- **Outcome**:

o   Bhishma's actions led to Amba's humiliation and her vow to seek revenge.

o   She later reincarnated as Shikhandi and played a pivotal role in Bhishma's death during the Kurukshetra War.

- **Impact**:

o   This swayamvara highlighted the darker side of patriarchal control and the consequences of disregarding a woman's autonomy.

4. Damayanti's Swayamvara (Nala-Damayanti Story)

- **Conditions**:

Damayanti, a princess, invited gods and men to her swayamvara. She chose Nala, a mortal king, despite the presence of divine suitors.

- **Stakeholders**:

o   **Damayanti**: The bride who exercised true autonomy.

o   **Nala**: The chosen suitor, known for his virtues.

o   **Gods**: Who tried to influence her choice?

- **Outcome**:

o   The swayamvara resulted in a deeply romantic union.

o   Despite later trials, their love and loyalty triumphed.

- **Impact**:

o   Damayanti's choice was a rare example of love and free will prevailing in a patriarchal setup.

Outcomes of Swayamvaras: Good and Bad

Positive Outcomes

1.   **Forging Alliances**:

Many swayamvaras strengthened political bonds between kingdoms.

2. **Meritocracy**:
They emphasized the importance of skill and character over wealth or brute force.

3. **Empowerment**:
Swayamvaras granted women a degree of autonomy in choosing their partners.

Negative Outcomes

1. **Wars and Rivalries**:

Failed suitors often retaliated, leading to conflicts and animosity.

2. **Exclusion and Injustice**:

Discrimination based on caste or status, as seen in Karna's disqualification, undermined the fairness of the process.

3. **Exploitation of Autonomy**:

Instances like Amba's swayamvara showed how women's choices were often overridden by patriarchal agendas.

Summary

The swayamvara tradition, while idealistic in concept, reflected the complexities of ancient Indian society, blending autonomy, merit, and socio-political motives.

While it empowered women to some extent, it also exposed societal flaws like caste discrimination and patriarchal control. Stories of famous swayamvaras continue to inspire, teach, and caution against the pitfalls of ego, discrimination, and the misuse of power.

Chapter Twenty Three - Some Untold Stories

Story of Matali, the celestial charioteer

Matali, the celestial charioteer of Indra, played a crucial role in aiding Lord Rama during his epic battle against Ravana in the Ramayana. When the devas led by Indra, realized the magnitude of the war and the necessity of divine intervention, Indra sent Matali to assist Rama. He arrived in a magnificent chariot, equipped with celestial weapons and drawn by divine horses that could traverse the skies and move at incredible speeds.

Matali's Contribution to Rama:

1.   Providing Indra's Chariot and Weapons:

Matali brought Indra's celestial chariot to Rama, which was designed for battles against formidable foes. The chariot was equipped with an array of divine weapons, including a powerful bow, inexhaustible arrows, an impenetrable shield, and a mighty spear. These were no ordinary tools but celestial armaments capable of countering Ravana's mystical and destructive arsenal.

2.   Guiding Rama in the Battle:

Matali's experience as Indra's charioteer made him an invaluable ally. He skillfully maneuvered the chariot through the battlefield, helping Rama counter Ravana's supernatural attacks. His deep understanding of battlefield tactics and his ability to interpret Ravana's strategies allowed Rama to anticipate and respond effectively to the demon king's maneuvers.

3. Encouragement and Advice:

As the battle intensified, Matali offered moral and strategic support to Rama. He reminded Rama to stay focused and utilize the divine weapons at the right moments. His guidance helped Rama remain composed during Ravana's relentless attacks and overwhelming illusions.

4. Countering Ravana's Illusions:

Ravana, known for his mastery of sorcery and deceptive tactics, unleashed illusions to confuse and overpower Rama. Matali, being a celestial figure with insight into such tricks, helped Rama see through the illusions, ensuring that he was not misled or defeated by Ravana's strategies.

5. Ensuring Swift Movement:

Matali's expert handling of the divine horses ensured that the chariot moved swiftly and seamlessly across the battlefield. This allowed Rama to dodge Ravana's attacks while positioning him advantageously to launch counterattacks.

Key Moments with Matali:

- **During the Climax:**

When Ravana summoned his most devastating weapons, Matali encouraged Rama to counter them with the celestial tools provided by Indra. It was under Matali's guidance that Rama used the Brahmastra, the ultimate weapon, to finally strike down Ravana.

- **Symbol of Divine Support:**

Matali's presence symbolized the heavens' support for Rama's cause, reinforcing the idea that Rama's mission to defeat Ravana was divinely ordained and backed by the cosmic order.

Through his expertise, courage, and divine resources, Matali ensured that Rama had every possible advantage against Ravana. His role exemplifies the harmony between divine intervention and human effort, highlighting the collaborative effort needed to overcome great challenges.

As the final battle between Lord Rama and the mighty demon king Ravana unfolded, the earth trembled, the sky darkened, and the heavens watched with bated breath. The clash was unlike any seen before, with the forces of good and evil colliding in a storm of divine and demonic powers.

The Arrival of Matali

In the midst of the chaos, when Rama needed divine support to match Ravana's celestial weapons, a sudden light pierced the battlefield. The luminous chariot of Indra descended from the skies, blazing with celestial radiance. It was driven by Matali, the renowned charioteer of Indra, who had come on the command of the king of gods to assist Rama in this decisive battle.

The chariot itself was a marvel of divine craftsmanship, adorned with golden embellishments and encrusted with dazzling gems. Its wheels spun with a sound that echoed through the heavens, and its reins controlled four celestial horses that could gallop across the skies and through dimensions. Matali, clad in resplendent attire, greeted Rama with folded hands, his voice resonant and filled with reverence.

"Lord Rama," he said, bowing deeply, "the gods have witnessed your unwavering valor and the righteousness of your cause. Indra, the king of the heavens, has sent his chariot and weapons to aid you in this righteous war. Use them to vanquish the evil Ravana and restore dharma to the world."

The Divine Armaments

Matali presented Rama with Indra's celestial weapons:

1.   **The Bow of Indra**: A magnificent weapon that could launch arrows imbued with the energy of the cosmos.

2.   **Inexhaustible Arrows**: These arrows, once fired, never missed their target and could pierce through any armor or illusion.

3.   **A Radiant Shield**: Forged in the celestial forges, the shield could repel even the deadliest of attacks.

4.   **The Spear of Thunder**: Capable of unleashing devastating energy that could obliterate anything in its path.

Rama, with gratitude in his heart, accepted the divine offerings and mounted the celestial chariot. As he stood tall, with his bow in hand and Matali at the reins, a divine glow surrounded him, instilling hope in his allies and fear in the hearts of Ravana's forces.

Matali's Tactical Brilliance

As Ravana's monstrous chariot, driven by ghastly steeds, rose into the air, Matali took charge, steering Indra's chariot with unparalleled skill. He weaved through Ravana's relentless assaults with such precision that Rama could focus entirely on countering the demon king's attacks.

•   When Ravana unleashed storms of fiery arrows and venomous serpents, Matali maneuvered the chariot with lightning speed, dodging the deadly onslaught.

•   He urged Rama to use specific weapons at the right time. "O Lord," he advised, "unleash Indra's spear now to counter Ravana's Agneyastra (fire weapon), for it alone can extinguish its blazing fury!"

Rama, trusting Matali's wisdom, acted swiftly, neutralizing Ravana's attack.

Conquering Ravana's Illusions

Ravana, realizing he was being outmatched, invoked his mastery over maya (illusion) to create decoys and conceal his true form. He multiplied himself on the battlefield, making it impossible to distinguish his real chariot from the fake ones. Matali, however, was no ordinary charioteer. With his celestial vision, he discerned the real Ravana amidst the illusions.

"Lord Rama," he called, pointing at a specific chariot hidden among the decoys, "there lies the true Ravana. Strike now, for this is your moment!" Rama, with his unerring aim, shot an arrow that destroyed the illusions and revealed Ravana's actual position.

The Decisive Moment

As the battle reached its climax, Ravana summoned his most powerful weapon, the Shakti Astra, capable of annihilating entire armies. The weapon surged toward Rama with unstoppable force. Matali's voice rang out, calm yet commanding: "Invoke the Brahmastra, Lord Rama. It is the only force in creation that can counter Ravana's wrath!"

Rama, standing tall in the chariot, raised the Brahmastra, a weapon of unparalleled destruction, and invoked its power. As the divine weapon soared toward Ravana, its brilliance outshone the sun, and its energy shook the three worlds. It struck Ravana with a force that shattered his arrogance and brought an end to his reign of terror.

The Aftermath

With Ravana defeated, the battlefield fell silent. Matali steered the chariot back to the ground, where Rama dismounted, his aura radiant with the triumph of dharma. Matali, bowing once again, said, "The heavens rejoice in your victory, Lord Rama. My task here is complete, and I shall return to Indra with the tale of your heroism."

With that, Matali ascended to the heavens, his chariot disappearing into the clouds, leaving behind a sense of divine intervention and the assurance that dharma had prevailed.

Story of Lord Rama, Sita and Kevat

The story of Lord Rama, Sita, and Kevat is one of the most touching episodes in the Ramayana, symbolizing devotion, humility, and divine grace. Kevat, a simple boatman, becomes a significant character when Rama, Sita, and Lakshmana reach the banks of the Ganga during their exile. This interaction beautifully illustrates the love and reverence ordinary devotees have for the divine and how the divine reciprocates with grace and humility.

The Setting

It was a serene evening on the banks of the Ganga. The river shimmered under the soft glow of the setting sun, its gentle waves lapping at the shore. Rama, Sita, and Lakshmana, weary from their journey, approached the river, seeking passage across. The peaceful environment mirrored the calm determination in Rama's heart as he continued his exile for the sake of dharma.

As they stood on the riverbank, a humble boatman named Kevat, clad in simple attire, noticed them from afar. His heart leaped with joy upon recognizing Rama, whom he revered deeply. Kevat hurried to the shore, his small boat swaying gently on the waters.

Kevat's Reverence

As Kevat approached, he prostrated himself before Rama and said, his voice trembling with devotion, "O

Lord, it is my great fortune to see you today. What service can this humble servant render to you?"

Rama, ever gentle and soft-spoken, smiled warmly and replied, "Dear Kevat, we need to cross this river. Could you kindly ferry us to the other side?"

Kevat, however, hesitated. With folded hands, he said, "Prabhu, I would be honored to ferry you, but I have one request. Allow me to wash your feet before you step into my boat."

Lakshmana, protective and practical, interjected, "Why do you need to wash my brother's feet? We are travelers with no wealth to give you. Let us cross the river without delay."

But Kevat, unshaken, humbly explained, "O Lakshmana, I have heard that the dust of Lord Rama's feet has the power to transform stones into living beings. If even a speck of that dust touches my boat, it might turn into a woman like Ahalya. How will a poor boatman like me earn his living then?"

The Washing of Feet

Rama, understanding Kevat's deep devotion and clever humility, agreed with a gentle nod. Kevat fetched a brass vessel filled with river water and, with reverence, knelt before Rama. Slowly, he washed the Lord's feet, his hands trembling as he felt the touch of divinity. The water he used became sacred, and Kevat sprinkled a few drops on his own head, feeling purified and blessed.

Sita, moved by Kevat's devotion, looked at him with a motherly smile, her eyes brimming with compassion. She said, "Kevat, your heart is pure, and your service to Rama will never be forgotten."

Crossing the Ganga

Once Kevat had washed Rama's feet, he guided them into his modest boat. As he rowed across the Ganga, Kevat's heart overflowed with joy. He gazed at Rama, his face radiant with humility, and said, "Prabhu, my life's purpose is fulfilled today. I am but a lowly boatman, yet you, the Lord of the universe, have graced my boat with your presence."

Rama, touched by Kevat's simplicity, replied, "Kevat, your love and devotion make you greater than the wealthiest of kings. You see me not as a prince but as the essence of your heart's devotion. For that, you will always remain close to me."

Kevat then turned to Sita and said, "Mother, you are the goddess of the universe, yet you tread these rough paths for the sake of dharma. Your sacrifice is unmatched, and it inspires simple men like me to remain steadfast in our duties."

Sita, her voice soft and nurturing, blessed Kevat, saying, "May your devotion to Rama bring you eternal peace and fulfillment."

Kevat's Farewell

Upon reaching the other shore, Kevat stepped out and bowed deeply before Rama, Sita, and Lakshmana. As they alighted from the boat, Kevat refused to accept any payment. "Prabhu," he said, "a boatman does not charge another boatman. Just as I have ferried you across this river, you must ferry me across the ocean of samsara (worldly existence). That is all I ask."

Rama, deeply moved by Kevat's pure-hearted devotion, placed his hand on Kevat's shoulder and said, "Your wish is granted, Kevat. When the time comes, I will ensure your liberation."

With tears streaming down his cheeks, Kevat watched as Rama, Sita, and Lakshmana disappeared into the forest, their figures bathed in the golden light of dusk. The sacred water where he had washed Rama's feet remained a symbol of divine grace, and Kevat's simple heart swelled with the knowledge that he had served the Lord in his own humble way.

Symbolism of the Episode

The encounter between Rama, Sita, and Kevat is not merely a literal crossing of the Ganga but also a spiritual allegory. Kevat's boat represents the journey across the ocean of life, and his selfless devotion highlights how humility and faith can bring one closer to divinity. Rama's acceptance of Kevat's service underscores the Lord's love for his devotees, regardless of their status or wealth.

This episode exemplifies the mutual love between the divine and the devotee, showing how even the simplest acts of service, when done with pure devotion, are cherished by the divine.

Sita's Gift to Kevat

As the divine trio Rama, Sita, and Lakshmana stepped onto the boat and Kevat began rowing across the Ganga, the journey was filled with a divine serenity. The ripples of the water mirrored the gentle rhythm of Kevat's oars, and the orange hues of the setting sun bathed the river in a golden glow.

Kevat, while concentrating on rowing, glanced occasionally at Rama and Sita with awe. He felt a deep sense of fulfillment in serving them. As they reached the other side of the river, Kevat helped them step out of the boat with utmost care and reverence.

Sita's Gesture of Gratitude

Sita, moved by Kevat's unwavering devotion and humility, decided to offer him something as a token of her gratitude. She reached into the folds of her saree and brought out a ring, a simple but elegant piece of jewelry she had kept as a personal treasure.

"Kevat," Sita said softly, her voice filled with maternal kindness, "you have served us selflessly and asked for nothing in return. Accept this humble gift from me as a blessing and remembrance of this moment."

Kevat, overwhelmed by the gesture, hesitated to take it. "Mother," he said, bowing his head, "your words are the greatest treasure I could ever receive. What use do I, a simple boatman, have for a precious ornament like this?"

But Sita insisted, placing the ring gently in his hand. "This is not merely gold, Kevat. It carries my heartfelt gratitude. Please accept it as a token of our appreciation for your service."

Kevat looked at the ring and then at Sita, his eyes brimming with tears. "If you wish me to accept it, I will, but I shall never use it for wealth or personal gain. I will keep it as a sacred blessing, a reminder of the day I had the honor of serving the divine."

Kevat's Humble Farewell

As Kevat folded his hands and stepped back, Rama, who had been quietly observing, spoke gently, "Kevat, your devotion is unparalleled. Sita's gift is a symbol of her love for all who serve with pure hearts. Keep it close, and it will guide you through life's challenges."

Kevat bowed low, touching his forehead to the ground, and said, "Prabhu, Mata, your blessings are all I need. If ever I falter in life, I will look to this moment for strength and faith."

He stood on the riverbank, watching as Rama, Sita, and Lakshmana disappeared into the forest, their divine aura slowly fading from sight. Holding the ring close to his heart, Kevat whispered a prayer of gratitude to the gods for granting him this rare opportunity.

Significance of Sita's Gift

The ring Sita gave to Kevat symbolizes her role as a compassionate mother figure, which always recognizes and honors devotion and service, no matter how humble. Kevat's humility in accepting the gift further highlights the virtues of gratitude and devotion, showing that even the smallest acts of service for the divine are met with grace and blessings.

Let's explore another beautiful and heartwarming episode from the Ramayana. One that stands out is the meeting of Lord Rama with **Shabari**, the elderly devotee who waited her entire life for his arrival. This interaction is a profound tale of devotion, patience, and the divine acknowledgment of a pure heart.

The Story of Rama and Shabari

The Setting

Deep in the forests of the Dandaka (Dandakaranya), where tall trees whispered ancient secrets and streams murmured soft tunes; lived an old woman named Shabari. Born into a tribal community, Shabari had dedicated her life to serving her guru, Sage Matanga. Before departing from the mortal world, the sage assured her that Lord Rama would one day visit her hut and bless her with his divine presence.

Years turned into decades as Shabari faithfully awaited Rama's arrival. Her love and devotion for him grew stronger with each passing day. Though old and frail, she would wake up early each morning, sweep her small hut, and gather berries to offer to Rama, carefully tasting each one to ensure they were sweet and unspoiled.

Rama's Arrival

One fateful day, as Shabari was performing her daily rituals, she sensed a divine energy approaching her humble abode. Emerging from the forest were Lord Rama and Lakshmana, their radiant presence lighting up the surroundings. Overwhelmed with joy, Shabari ran to greet them, her frail hands trembling as she folded them in reverence.

"Prabhu, you have finally graced this unworthy servant's home," she exclaimed, tears streaming down her face. "All these years, I have waited for this moment. My life's purpose is fulfilled."

Rama, ever humble, smiled warmly and said, "Mother, your devotion has drawn me here. It is you who honor me with your love."

Shabari's offering

Shabari invited Rama and Lakshmana into her hut and offered them a seat on simple mats made of woven grass. With great care, she brought forth a leaf filled with berries. Before offering them, she confessed, "Prabhu, I tasted each berry to ensure they are sweet and worthy of you. Forgive me if this act offends you."

Lakshmana hesitated, but Rama, recognizing her pure devotion, took a berry and ate it with a smile. "Mother, your love has made these berries sweeter than nectar. There is no greater offering than one made with such sincerity."

Shabari's heart swelled with joy as she watched Rama eat. "My Lord," she said, her voice trembling, "I am but an unlettered woman from a humble background. Yet you, the Lord of the universe, accept my offering, what more could I ever desire?"

Their Conversation

As they spoke, Shabari shared the wisdom she had gained from her guru, emphasizing the importance of devotion, humility, and service. Rama, in turn, blessed her, saying, "Mother, your life is a testament to the power of faith. Those who approach the divine with a pure heart, as you have, are sure to attain liberation."

Shabari's Enlightenment

As Shabari sat before Rama, she expressed her gratitude and humbly asked for his guidance. Rama, pleased with her unwavering faith, imparted to her the principles of Navavidha Bhakti, the nine fold path of devotion:

1. **Listening to the stories of the divine.**

2. **Singing the praises of the divine.**

3. **Remembering the divine.**

4. **Serving the divine.**

5. **Worshipping with devotion.**

6. **Bowing with humility.**

7. **Acting as a servant of the divine.**

8. **Cultivating friendship with the divine.**

9. **Completely surrendering oneself to the divine.**

Rama explained that anyone who follows this path with a pure heart can attain liberation, regardless of their caste, gender, or status.

Shabari then directed Rama and Lakshmana toward the path that would lead them to Sugriva, where they would find help in their quest to rescue Sita.

Shabari's Liberation

After Rama and Lakshmana departed, Shabari's heart was filled with peace and fulfillment. She lit a sacred fire, meditated upon Rama's divine form, and merged with the eternal light, attaining liberation.

Significance of the Episode

The story of Shabari teaches us that devotion is not bound by social status, education, or rituals. Her simple act of tasting the berries for Rama shows that it is the purity of intent that matters most to the divine. Rama's acceptance of her offering highlights his universal love and the truth that he values the heart behind the act over the act itself.

This episode continues to inspire millions, reminding us that the divine responds to sincere love and devotion, regardless of how small or simple the offering may seem.

Here's another cherished episode from the Ramayana that highlights deep devotion, humility, and the unbreakable bond of service, **The Story of Hanuman's Search for Sita in Lanka**.

Hanuman's Search for Sita

The Divine Mission

After meeting Lord Rama at Kishkindha, Hanuman swore an oath of unwavering service to his lord. When Rama handed him his ring as a token to identify himself to Sita, Hanuman felt deeply honored. His heart brimmed with determination to fulfill his mission: to find Sita, imprisoned in Ravana's golden city, Lanka, and bring back news of her safety.

Carrying Rama's blessings and his divine strength, Hanuman leaped across the vast ocean to reach Lanka. The journey itself was perilous, with challenges such as Mainaka Mountain, Surasa the serpent, and the demoness Simhika, all of which Hanuman overcame with his wits, strength, and faith in Rama.

Hanuman's First Glimpse of Sita

After reaching Lanka, Hanuman shrunk to the size of a tiny monkey and began exploring Ravana's opulent city. The grandeur of Lanka dazzled him, but he remained focused on his goal.

He finally found Sita in Ashok Vatika, sitting under a large Ashoka tree. Her appearance was radiant despite her sorrow. She was thin and pale, her face etched with grief, yet she emanated an aura of divine dignity. She sat amidst the demonesses who guarded her, weeping softly, her thoughts consumed by Rama.

Hanuman's Conversation with Sita

Hanuman hid in the branches of the tree, observing her with reverence. He decided to reveal himself carefully, for sudden contact might alarm her. Gently, he began reciting verses praising Lord Rama. Sita, startled but hopeful, looked up and saw the tiny monkey who spoke of her beloved.

Hanuman descended and bowed before her. "Mother," he said humbly, "I am Hanuman, a servant of Lord Rama. He has sent me to find you and assure you of his arrival to rescue you."

Tears of relief streamed down Sita's face. "Hanuman," she said, "you are a blessing from Rama. Tell him I wait for him every moment, clinging to the hope of our reunion."

Hanuman gave her Rama's ring as proof of his identity. Sita held it close to her heart, her spirits lifted by the thought of Rama's love and determination.

Sita's Gift to Hanuman

As a token of gratitude and to convey her message, Sita gave Hanuman a jewel from her hair. "Take this to my lord," she said, her voice trembling with emotion. "It will remind him of our bond and give him strength to endure the trials ahead."

Hanuman accepted the jewel with reverence, bowing deeply. "Mother, your words and your strength inspire me. I swear upon Rama's name that I will deliver this safely and return with him to rescue you."

Hanuman's Mighty Feats in Lanka

Before leaving, Hanuman decided to observe Ravana and his court to gauge their strength. Disguised again, he infiltrated the palace and witnessed Ravana's arrogance. To make his presence known, Hanuman allowed himself to be captured after causing havoc in the Ashok Vatika. Dragged to Ravana's court, Hanuman boldly declared Rama's greatness and warned the demon king of his impending doom.

When Ravana ordered his tail to be set ablaze, Hanuman used the fire to burn down large parts of Lanka before leaping back across the ocean to deliver Sita's message and jewel to Rama.

Significance of the Episode

Hanuman's journey to Lanka showcases his unparalleled devotion, courage, and humility. His interactions with Sita reflect his role not just as a messenger but as a source of comfort and hope for her during her darkest times. The jewel symbolizes the unbroken bond between Rama and Sita, serving as a tangible reminder of their love and faith in each other.

This episode teaches us that true service comes from selflessness, unwavering faith, and the courage to overcome all obstacles in devotion to a higher purpose.

Here's another cherished episode from the Ramayana, **The Bond Between Bharat and Rama**. This story beautifully illustrates sibling love, duty, and sacrifice, showcasing the ideals of Dharma in the most poignant way.

The Bond between Bharat and Rama

Bharat's Discovery of the Exile

When Bharat returned to Ayodhya after his visit to his maternal grandparents, he found the city enveloped in gloom. His heart sank as he learned the shocking truth: his mother, Kaikeyi, had manipulated King Dasharatha into sending Rama into exile and securing the throne for him. Devastated by his mother's actions and grieving his father's death, Bharat rejected the throne outright.

"My brother Rama is the rightful king," Bharat declared. "I shall not take what is not mine by Dharma."

Determined to bring Rama back, Bharat, accompanied by his mothers, priests, and citizens of Ayodhya, set out for the forest where Rama, Sita, and Lakshmana had taken refuge.

The Emotional Reunion

In Chitrakoot, where Rama was living a life of simplicity, Bharat arrived with his entourage. As Rama and Lakshmana heard the commotion, they wondered if Ayodhya had sent soldiers to bring them back by force. But when Bharat approached, his face tear-streaked and his posture humble, Rama immediately embraced him.

The two brothers wept together, their bond unbroken despite the distance and events that had transpired.

"Brother," Bharat cried, "I have come to take you back. Ayodhya is incomplete without you. The throne belongs to you alone, as ordained by Dharma."

Rama, calm and resolute, replied, "Dear Bharat, I know your heart. But our father's word is supreme. I must honor his promise and fulfill my exile."

Bharat's Plea

Bharat fell at Rama's feet. "If you will not return, then let me join you in the forest. I cannot bear to rule without you by my side. The people of Ayodhya long for your leadership not mine."

Rama lifted his brother and said with compassion, "Bharat, you are as worthy as I am to rule. The people need a king to guide them. You must return to Ayodhya and serve them as I would. This is your Dharma now."

Rama's Gift to Bharat

Seeing Bharat's despair, Rama gave him his sandals. "Place these on the throne," he said. "Let them serve as a symbol of my rule. Rule in my name, and consider yourself a custodian of Ayodhya until I return."

Bharat accepted the sandals with great reverence, tears streaming down his face. "I shall place these sandals on the throne and live as a servant, awaiting your return. My every decision will honor your values and guidance."

Bharat's Life in Nandigram

True to his word, Bharat returned to Ayodhya but refused to live in the palace. Instead, he moved to Nandigram, a village near Ayodhya, where he led an ascetic life, dressing in simple clothes and eating only what was necessary. The throne of Ayodhya remained unoccupied, with Rama's sandals placed upon it as a divine reminder of his eventual return.

Every day, Bharat prayed for Rama's safety and waited for the day his elder brother would return to reclaim the kingdom.

Significance of the Episode

The relationship between Rama and Bharat highlights the ideal bond between siblings, rooted in love, respect, and shared responsibility. Bharat's selflessness and Rama's unwavering commitment to Dharma are timeless examples of duty and sacrifice.

This episode teaches us that true leadership lies in humility and that love for family and adherence to Dharma are the highest virtues one can uphold.

Here's another significant and emotionally resonant episode from the Ramayana: **The Episode of Jatayu's Sacrifice**. This story highlights courage, devotion, and the ultimate sacrifice for a righteous cause.

Jatayu's Encounter with Ravana

The Abduction of Sita

As Ravana carried Sita away in his golden chariot, the skies trembled with her cries for help. Her heart pined for Rama, and she called upon the birds and animals of the forest to bear witness to her abduction. It was then that Jatayu, the great vulture king and a dear friend of Dasharatha, heard her desperate plea.

Although old and frail, Jatayu's heart burned with a sense of duty to protect Sita, the beloved wife of Rama. With unwavering resolve, he soared into the sky, intercepting Ravana's chariot.

Jatayu Confronts Ravana

"Ravana you vile king!" Jatayu roared. "How dare you abduct a noble woman like Sita? Do you not know that Lord Rama will bring justice upon you for this heinous act? Release her now, or face my wrath!"

Ravana sneered, his arrogance unshaken. "Old bird, do you think you can stop me? My power is unmatched. Stand aside or you shall meet your end."

But Jatayu refused to relent. With fierce determination, he attacked Ravana, clawing at his chariot and tearing apart its canopy. The two engaged in a fierce aerial battle, with Jatayu striking Ravana with his talons and beak, all the while urging Sita not to lose hope.

Jatayu's Sacrifice

Despite his valor, Jatayu was no match for Ravana's strength and celestial weapons. The demon king struck Jatayu with his sword, leaving him mortally wounded. The vulture fell to the ground, his wings shattered, yet his spirit remained unbroken.

Before Ravana flew away with Sita, Jatayu called out to her, "Do not despair, my child. Rama will come for you. He will defeat this tyrant and bring you back."

Rama and Lakshmana Find Jatayu

As Rama and Lakshmana searched the forest for Sita, they stumbled upon the dying Jatayu. The sight of the noble bird, lying in a pool of blood, filled them with grief. Rama knelt beside him, cradling his head.

"Jatayu my father's friend, who harmed you like this?" Rama asked, his voice trembling.

With his last breaths, Jatayu recounted the events, describing how he tried to stop Ravana and how Sita had been taken southward toward Lanka. Tears streamed down Rama's face as he realized the depth of Jatayu's sacrifice.

"Jatayu," Rama said, his voice choked with emotion, "you have shown unparalleled bravery and devotion. You will be remembered for eternity as a noble soul who gave his life for Dharma."

Jatayu's Liberation

As Jatayu breathed his last, Rama performed his final rites with great reverence, treating him like a father. He lit a pyre for the noble bird, granting him moksha (liberation) through his divine touch.

Significance of the Episode

The episode of Jatayu's sacrifice is a poignant reminder of the courage it takes to stand against injustice, even in the face of certain death. Jatayu's selfless act of protecting Sita embodies the essence of Dharma: to fight for what is right, regardless of one's limitations or fears.

For Rama, this encounter deepened his resolve to rescue Sita and punish Ravana, while also highlighting the profound bonds of loyalty and love that transcend species and status.

Chapter Twenty Four - Great Leap of Hanuman and Burning of Lanka

Here's another profound and inspiring episode from the Ramayana: **Hanuman's Leap to Lanka**. This story showcases Hanuman's unparalleled devotion, strength, and intelligence as he embarks on a mission to locate Sita in Ravana's kingdom.

The Call for a Hero

Rama's Command

After Rama and Lakshmana formed an alliance with the monkey king Sugriva, they sent search parties in all directions to locate Sita. Hanuman, the trusted servant of Sugriva and a devoted follower of Rama, was tasked with traveling south. Guided by Sampati, Jatayu's elder brother, Hanuman learned that Sita was being held captive in Lanka.

The challenge lay in crossing the vast ocean that separated India from Lanka. The Vanara army stood at the shore, pondering how to accomplish this impossible task. Hanuman, however, was destined for greatness.

Realizing His Potential

Jambuvan, the wise bear-king, reminded Hanuman of his forgotten powers. Hanuman had been blessed with immense strength, agility, and intelligence, but a curse had veiled his awareness of these abilities until needed. Upon hearing Jambuvan's words, Hanuman's confidence surged. He grew to an enormous size, his resolve firm to fulfill Rama's mission.

"I will find Sita, and I will return with news of her safety," Hanuman declared, bowing to Rama before leaping into the skies.

Hanuman's Leap across the Ocean

Encounters during the Journey

As Hanuman soared across the ocean, his journey was fraught with challenges:

1.   **Mainaka Mountain:** The Mountain Mainaka rose from the ocean to offer Hanuman rest, reminding him of his divine ancestry and offering gratitude for his mission. However, Hanuman politely declined, stating, "I cannot rest until I have fulfilled my Lord's mission."

2.   **Surasa, the Serpent Mother:** To test his determination, the sea goddess Surasa blocked his path, demanding he enter her mouth. Hanuman cleverly shrank his size, darted through her mouth, and emerged victorious, earning her blessings.

3.   **Simhika, the Shadow-Demoness:** A demoness tried to capture Hanuman by seizing his shadow. Hanuman swiftly attacked and vanquished her, continuing his journey undeterred.

Arrival in Lanka

A City of Splendor and Sin

As Hanuman reached Lanka, he marveled at its beauty. Ravana's golden city gleamed under the moonlight, its grandeur a stark contrast to the darkness of its ruler's deeds. Hanuman shrank to the size of a cat to move unnoticed.

At the city gates, he encountered **Lankini**, the guardian spirit of Lanka, who attempted to stop him. With a single blow, Hanuman defeated her. Lankini, realizing his divine mission, bowed and said, "This marks the beginning of Ravana's downfall."

Finding Sita

Hanuman searched through Ravana's palace and gardens, finally locating Sita in the Ashoka Vatika. She sat beneath a tree, her face pale with sorrow but her heart resolute in loyalty to Rama. Overwhelmed by her grief Hanuman waited until she was alone to reveal himself.

The Meeting with Sita

Hanuman approached Sita with great reverence, introducing himself as Rama's messenger. To gain her trust, he presented her with Rama's ring, a token of his love and reassurance. Sita's eyes filled with tears as she clutched the ring.

"Tell my lord," she said, "that I await him with unwavering faith. Let him come soon, for my heart cannot bear this separation much longer."

Moved by her devotion, Hanuman promised her that Rama would come to rescue her. Before leaving, he offered her a piece of advice: "Keep your courage, for the day of Ravana's doom is near."

Hanuman's Valor in Lanka

Before departing, Hanuman decided to assess Ravana's strength. Allowing himself to be captured, he was brought before Ravana, where he boldly warned the demon king of his impending defeat. "Release Sita and seek forgiveness, or face the wrath of Rama," Hanuman declared.

Ravana, enraged, ordered that Hanuman's tail be set on fire. However, Hanuman used this as an opportunity. Growing to an enormous size, he set the entire city ablaze with his fiery tail, sparing Ashoka Vatika, where Sita resided and Bibhishan's palace.

Chapter Twenty Five - Hanuman's Return to Rama

With his mission complete, Hanuman leaped back across the ocean and delivered the joyous news to Rama. "Sita is safe and steadfast in her devotion to you," he said. Rama's heart swelled with gratitude for Hanuman's courage and loyalty.

Significance of the Episode

The episode of Hanuman's leap to Lanka demonstrates the power of devotion and the potential within every individual to achieve greatness. Hanuman's unwavering focus on Rama's mission, his courage in the face of danger, and his intelligence in overcoming challenges make him a symbol of faith, strength, and selfless service.

Let's delve into another thrilling episode from the Ramayana: **The Burning of Lanka,** a dramatic and pivotal moment that showcases Hanuman's unmatched bravery and devotion to Lord Rama.

Prelude to the Blaze

After meeting Sita and delivering Rama's message, Hanuman's heart was filled with pride and purpose. Yet, before leaving Lanka, he decided to assess Ravana's power and create fear among the demons, thus laying the groundwork for Rama's eventual victory. Hanuman knew this would strengthen Sita's hope and warn Ravana of the consequences of his actions.

The Court of Ravana

As part of his plan, Hanuman allowed himself to be captured by Ravana's soldiers after causing havoc in the Ashoka Vatika by uprooting trees, destroying demon guards, and challenging Ravana's authority.

Bound with ropes, Hanuman was taken to Ravana's court. Despite his captivity, he stood tall and fearless before the mighty king.

Ravana glared at Hanuman and roared, "Who are you, monkey, and why have you dared to wreak havoc in my kingdom?"

Hanuman responded with calm confidence, "I am a humble servant of Lord Rama, who is the epitome of virtue and righteousness. I have come as his messenger, warning you to return Sita or face destruction."

Ravana, enraged by Hanuman's audacity, ordered his execution. However, Ravana's wise brother Bibhishan intervened, reminding Ravana of the code of ethics, which prohibited killing an emissary.

Instead, Ravana decreed, "Set his tail on fire. Let him suffer and serve as a warning to others who dare to oppose me!"

Hanuman's Fiery Resolve

The demons wrapped Hanuman's tail in layers of cloth soaked in oil and set it ablaze. Instead of succumbing to fear or pain, Hanuman chanted Rama's name and grew to an enormous size. He leaped out of captivity, leaving the demons dumbfounded.

With his tail ablaze, Hanuman soared across the city, using the fire as a weapon. He leaped from palace to palace, setting Ravana's golden Lanka aflame.

The flames engulfed the city, turning its grandeur into ashes. Ravana's mighty fortresses, palaces, and armories were reduced to ruins. The demons ran in terror, crying out for help. Despite the destruction, Hanuman ensured that no harm came to Sita or the Ashoka Vatika.

Sita's Protection and Hanuman's Reflection

After ensuring Sita's safety, Hanuman flew to the ocean to extinguish the fire on his tail. As he gazed at the burning city from a distance, he reflected on the devastation he had caused. For a moment, he worried that Sita might have been harmed, but his heart found solace in the thought that Rama's mission had been furthered.

A Final Bow to Sita

Before leaving Lanka, Hanuman returned to Sita. He bowed before her and said, "Mother, I have shown Ravana a glimpse of Rama's power. Stay strong, for your lord will soon come to rescue you."

Sita blessed Hanuman. Her heart filled with gratitude and renewed hope. She gave him a jewel from her hair as a token for Rama, asking him to convey her steadfast devotion and longing.

The Return to Rama

Hanuman leaped across the ocean back to Rama and the Vanara army. He narrated the events in Lanka, describing Sita's unyielding resolve and his daring exploits. Presenting Sita's jewel to Rama, he said, "She awaits you, my Lord, and her faith in you remains unshaken."

Rama, overwhelmed with emotion, embraced Hanuman and praised him for his courage, loyalty, and ingenuity. "You have accomplished what no one else could," Rama said, "and your actions have strengthened our path to victory."

Significance of the Episode

The burning of Lanka is one of the most iconic moments in the Ramayana. It symbolizes the triumph of devotion and righteousness over arrogance and evil. Hanuman's fearless actions not only humbled Ravana but also inspired Rama and his allies. This episode highlights Hanuman's extraordinary qualities:

- **Unwavering Faith:** Hanuman's devotion to Rama gave him the strength to overcome any obstacle.

- **Strategic Intelligence:** His decision to burn Lanka was not just an act of destruction but a calculated move to weaken Ravana's confidence.

- **Selfless Service:** Every action of Hanuman was aimed at fulfilling Rama's mission and reassuring Sita of her imminent rescue.

Let's explore the next significant chapter of the Ramayana: **The Building of the Rama Setu**—the bridge to Lanka, which showcases the determination, teamwork, and divine intervention that marked Rama's mission to rescue Sita.

Chapter Twenty Six - The Vanara Army at the Ocean

Reaching the Shores of the Southern Sea

After Hanuman's triumphant return and report, Rama, Lakshmana, and the Vanara army marched south toward Lanka. They reached the vast shores of the ocean, which separated them from Ravana's golden city. Standing before the endless waters, Rama realized they had to cross this immense barrier to reach Lanka.

The sight of the ocean brought a moment of contemplation. The waves roared, reflecting the immense challenge ahead. Rama, determined to find a way, decided to seek the ocean's assistance.

Rama's Appeal to the Ocean God

A Plea for Passage

Rama sat in meditation on the shore, praying to Samudra, the Ocean God, to grant safe passage for his army. For three days and nights, Rama pleaded with unwavering patience. However, the ocean remained silent, testing the resolve of the divine prince.

Rama's Wrath

On the fourth day, Rama's patience turned into righteous anger. Determined to take matters into his own hands, he took up his celestial bow and aimed fiery arrows at the ocean, threatening to dry it up. The sea trembled at Rama's might, and waves surged in fear.

Suddenly, the Ocean God emerged, bowing before Rama. "Forgive my silence, my Lord," he said. "It is my nature to remain bound by laws. I cannot dry myself or part on my own. However, I shall support your efforts to cross. Build a bridge, and I will hold it steady."

The Construction of Rama Setu

Nala and the Vanaras

Nala, a skilled Vanara and the son of the divine architect Vishwakarma, stepped forward. "I possess the knowledge of construction," he said. "With the strength of our army and the blessings of Rama, we shall build a bridge that no storm can break."

The Vanaras sprang into action, lifting massive boulders, trees, and stones. Each rock was inscribed with the name of Rama, a detail that turned the construction into an act of devotion. Miraculously, the rocks floated upon the water, held steady by the Ocean God's promise.

The Power of Teamwork

Thousands of Vanaras worked tirelessly. Hanuman lifted mountains and carried them to the shore. Sugriva and Angada organized the labor, ensuring that every part of the bridge was strong and secure. Rama and Lakshmana inspired the workers with their presence, encouraging them with words of hope and gratitude.

Day by day, the bridge grew longer, stretching across the sea toward Lanka. The sight of the bridge uplifted the spirits of the Vanaras, who chanted Rama's name with each stone they placed.

Divine Intervention

Floating Rocks and Miracles

The inscription of Rama's name on the rocks was not merely symbolic; it imbued the stones with divine energy. Even the smallest pebble became weightless and buoyant when blessed by the Lord's name. This miracle reaffirmed the faith of the Vanaras and highlighted the power of devotion.

Hanuman's Leap of Faith

As the bridge neared completion, Hanuman tested its strength by leaping from one end to the other. The structure held firm, a testament to the unity and faith of the army. "This bridge is not merely built of stone," Hanuman said, "but of the unwavering devotion of every Vanara here."

Crossing the Bridge

After days of effort, the Rama Setu stood complete, a marvel of engineering and devotion. Rama stood at the edge of the bridge, his heart filled with gratitude for the efforts of his allies and the blessings of the divine.

As the army crossed the bridge, they sang songs of victory, their voices resonating across the ocean. Rama, walking alongside Lakshmana, silently vowed to end Ravana's tyranny and restore righteousness.

Significance of the Rama Setu

1. **A Symbol of Faith and Devotion:** The Bridge was not just a physical structure but a manifestation of the collective devotion and determination of Rama's allies.

2. **The Power of Unity:** The Vanaras, though seemingly ordinary, achieved the extraordinary through teamwork and trust in their leader.

3. **Divine Blessings:** The floating stones inscribed with Rama's name symbolize the miracles that occur when faith and action align.

4. **A Testament to Leadership:** Rama's ability to inspire unwavering loyalty and effort among his allies underscored his role as an ideal leader.

Prelude to the War

With the Rama Setu complete, the Vanara army stood poised to invade Lanka. The bridge became a path not just to the enemy's stronghold but to the fulfillment of Rama's mission. Ravana, watching from his golden palace, realized that his time was running out.

Chapter Twenty Seven - The Battle of Lanka

This chapter is divided into two parts. *Part One* devotes to the fact that Ravan's Lanka was so protected that not even Hanuman could break its security system. At the same time today's context of women's empowerment was relevant in Ravan's Lanka. *Part Two* devotes more on the battle between two armies.

Part One

Ravana's kingdom, Lanka, was known for its advanced security system, which reflected his strategic brilliance as a ruler. This system blended military prowess with mysticism, demonstrating his command over both worldly and supernatural domains.

Ravana's Kingdom Security System

1.   **Impenetrable   Architecture**: Lanka was constructed by Vishwakarma, the divine architect, using gold and other precious materials. Its design featured towering walls, guarded gates, and strategic layouts that made invasion nearly impossible.

2.   **Multi-layered Defenses**:

o   **Asura Army**: Ravana's army consisted of powerful rakshasas trained in combat and mystical arts.

o   **Magical Barriers**: Enchanted barriers and mantras protected Lanka from aerial and terrestrial attacks.

o   **Naval Strength**: Lanka, being an island kingdom, had a strong navy patrolling its waters.

3.   **Guardianship**:

Ravana delegated security to capable and trusted individuals, including mystical beings like Surasa and Lankini.

Surasa, Lankini and Trijata

Surasa: The Unyielding Protector of Lanka's Water and Air Security

Surasa, a prominent rakshasi in the *Ramayana*, exemplified a unique blend of power, strategy, and responsibility as the guardian of Lanka's air and water boundaries. Her role is particularly noteworthy, as it highlights the capability of women in leadership and defense roles, resonating strongly with the ideals of women's empowerment today.

Surasa's Role in Lanka's Security

1.   **Guardian of Air and Water Spaces**:

o   Surasa was tasked by Ravana with the formidable responsibility of ensuring that no unauthorized entity could penetrate Lanka's airspace or waterways.

o   Her vigilance was legendary—"not even a fly" could escape her scrutiny or bypass her watchful eyes. She embodied the principles of impenetrable defense and tactical surveillance.

o   She was not just a protector but also a symbol of Ravana's trust in women to hold critical positions in his kingdom's defense infrastructure.

2.   **Testing Hanuman's Resolve**:

o   Surasa famously tested Lord Hanuman when he was crossing the ocean to reach Lanka in search of Sita. She transformed into a gigantic form, blocking his path and challenging him to prove his worth.

o   This encounter demonstrated her strategic thinking and dedication to her duties, ensuring that only those deserving and determined could pass.

3.   **Master of Strategy**:

o   Her ability to challenge even someone as capable as Hanuman underscored her tactical brilliance. She balanced duty and dharma, ultimately allowing Hanuman to proceed once he proved his intentions were honorable.

Relating Surasa's Role to Modern Women's Empowerment

Surasa's role as a high-ranking security leader in Lanka reflects a progressive acknowledgment of women's abilities in critical and strategic domains. Drawing parallels to today's world, her story provides valuable lessons for women's empowerment:

1.   **Leadership in Defense and Security**:

o   Surasa's position as the protector of Lanka's water and air spaces highlights how women can lead in defense roles, much like modern-day women serving as commanders, pilots, and naval officers in various countries.

o   Today, women are excelling in roles within the military, cybersecurity, and border protection, breaking stereotypes about their capabilities in traditionally male-dominated sectors.

2.   **The Balance Between Strength and Wisdom:**

o   Surasa combined her physical strength with strategic intelligence. This mirrors how empowered women today are leading not just with force but also with sharp minds in diplomacy, defense policies, and crisis management.

3.   **Trust in Women's Potential:**

o   Ravana's entrustment of such a crucial role to Surasa signifies a belief in her capabilities. Similarly, modern societies are increasingly recognizing women's potential, placing them in positions of power and responsibility in governance, science, and defense.

4.   **Role Model for Aspiring Women:**

o   Surasa's story serves as an inspiration for young women aspiring to break barriers in security, technology, and leadership, proving that gender is no limitation to competence and excellence.

Surasa's role as the guardian of Lanka's air and water demonstrates a profound respect for women's abilities in leadership, strategy, and defense. Her example resonates with today's vision of women's empowerment, showcasing how women can and should be entrusted with critical roles. Like Surasa, modern women are breaking boundaries, asserting their presence in every domain, and proving that determination and skill transcend gender barriers.

- **Lankini**:

Lankini was the guardian spirit of Lanka, a celestial being cursed to serve as Lanka's protector. She ensured no intruder could enter without permission. However, when Hanuman reached Lanka, Lankini tried to stop him but was defeated. This incident marked the end of her curse, and she blessed Hanuman, signifying divine intervention in Lanka's fate.

Lankini: The Fearless Guardian of Lanka's Land

Lankini, the chief of land security in the city of Lanka during Ravana's reign, was a rakshasi of formidable strength and unwavering loyalty. Her role was pivotal in ensuring that no intruder breached the terrestrial boundaries of Lanka, a kingdom renowned for its impenetrable defenses and strategic fortifications. Lankini's fearless dedication to her duty and her willingness to sacrifice her life for the security of her homeland reflect her unparalleled commitment and determination.

Role and Responsibilities of Lankini

1.   **Chief of Land Security**:

o   Lankini served as the guardian of the gates of Lanka, controlling access to the island's interior. She was the first line of defense against any invaders or unauthorized entrants.

o   Her presence symbolized the strength and invulnerability of Lanka's security system under Ravana's rule.

2.   **Unyielding Protector of Lanka's Borders**:

o   Lankini's vigilance ensured that no one could enter Lanka unnoticed or without facing her scrutiny. She confronted intruders with unwavering determination, exemplifying her readiness to defend her kingdom at all costs.

3.   **Encounter with Hanuman**:

o   When Hanuman entered Lanka in search of Sita, Lankini was the first to confront him. She challenged him with immense courage, displaying her loyalty and fearlessness in fulfilling her duty.

o   Despite her immense strength, she was eventually overpowered by Hanuman, who struck her with his mighty fist. Even in defeat, Lankini exhibited grace and wisdom, recognizing the divine will in Hanuman's mission.

4.   **Sacrifice and Wisdom**:

o   Lankini's willingness to face death while protecting Lanka's gates underscores her selfless devotion to her duty. Her bravery and acceptance of destiny reflect her deep understanding of dharma and the inevitability of Ravana's downfall.

o   After her defeat, Lankini provided Hanuman with valuable information, demonstrating her wisdom and integrity even in adversity.

Lankini's Determination and Fearlessness

Lankini's role as the chief guardian of Lanka's land was marked by her:

1.   **Unwavering Loyalty**:

o   Her loyalty to Ravana and her homeland was absolute. She carried out her duties with diligence, embodying the ideals of dedication and patriotism.

2.   **Readiness for Sacrifice**:

o   Lankini was prepared to lay down her life in the line of duty. Her readiness to confront Hanuman, despite his evident strength, exemplifies her courage and fearlessness.

3.   **Symbol of Strength**:

o   Lankini's presence at the gates of Lanka symbolized the might and discipline of Ravana's reign. Her strength and determination were a testament to the invincibility of Lanka's defenses.

Legacy of Lankini

1.   **A Model of Duty and Devotion**:

o   Lankini's unwavering commitment to her responsibilities serves as a timeless example of duty and devotion. She stood as a protector of her land, embodying the principles of dharma even in challenging circumstances.

2.   **Wisdom in Defeat**:

o   Recognizing Hanuman's divine mission and the inevitability of Ravana's downfall, Lankini's acceptance of her defeat displayed her insight and grace. Her actions hinted at the moral complexities within Ravana's kingdom, where some individuals upheld righteousness despite their allegiance to the king.

Relating Lankini's Role to Modern Women's Empowerment

Lankini's role as the chief of security in Lanka resonates with the ideals of women's empowerment today:

1.   **Women in Defense and Security**:

o   Like Lankini, women today are increasingly taking on critical roles in national defense and security. From military commanders to intelligence officers, women are proving their mettle in protecting their nations.

2.   **Strength and Sacrifice**:

o   Lankini's readiness to sacrifice her life mirrors the courage and selflessness of women in modern defense forces, who face dangers and challenges with unwavering resolve.

3.   **Wisdom and Leadership**:

o   Lankini's actions reflect the balance of strength and wisdom that women bring to leadership roles, whether in security, governance, or community defense.

Lankini's role as the chief of land security for Lanka stands as a powerful example of dedication, fearlessness, and duty. Her willingness to sacrifice her life for her homeland and her wisdom in recognizing divine will make her a remarkable figure in the *Ramayana*. In today's context, Lankini symbolizes the strength, courage, and leadership that women bring to roles of responsibility and protection, inspiring generations to embrace these qualities in the pursuit of justice and security.

Trijata's Role in Lanka's Internal Security

Trijata, a rakshasi in the *Ramayana*, played a significant yet subtle role in maintaining internal security within Ravana's palace, especially in the Ashoka Vatika where Sita was held captive. Known for her wisdom and loyalty to dharma, Trijata stood out among the rakshasis for her compassionate and rational nature.

Key Contributions to Internal Security

1.   **Mediator Between Sita and the Rakshasis**:

o   Trijata served as a calming influence, ensuring that the more aggressive rakshasis guarding Sita did not harm or excessively torment her.

o   By maintaining order and discipline among the guards, she prevented potential chaos that could have undermined Ravana's control.

2.   **Advisor and Spy for Sita's Safety**:

o   Trijata frequently advised Sita to remain calm and steadfast in her devotion to Rama, indirectly securing her mental and emotional well-being.

o   Her dreams and warnings to the rakshasis about Ravana's downfall dissuaded them from harming Sita, maintaining internal stability in a volatile environment.

3.   **Loyal to Dharma Over Ravana**:

o   While serving Ravana's court, Trijata's loyalty to dharma made her an advocate for peace and reason.

o   She acted as an unofficial internal monitor, ensuring that Ravana's excessive ambitions did not result in further injustices.

4.   **Guardian of Secrets**:

o   Trijata was privy to sensitive information, including Sita's interactions and the strategies of Ravana's inner circle.

o   Her discretion and wisdom ensured that critical information was neither leaked to Ravana's enemies prematurely nor misused within Lanka.

Significance of Her Role:

Trijata's position as a senior rakshasi with a moral compass made her a stabilizing force in Ravana's otherwise tyrannical and tumultuous reign. Her subtle acts of defiance and protection contributed to Sita's safety and hinted at the presence of ethical resistance even within Lanka's ranks.

How Were These Women Assigned Security Duties?

The roles of Surasa and Lankini were granted based on their exceptional abilities.

• Ravana, a strategic ruler, valued competence over gender, assigning duties to those best suited for the task.

• Lankini's position was divinely ordained due to her curse, while Surasa earned her role through loyalty and skill.

Women's Empowerment in the Ramayana

The epic portrays women in diverse roles, from warriors and advisors to spiritual guides and nurturers, reflecting a nuanced approach to women's empowerment. This legacy inspired societies in ancient India and Southeast Asia to value women's leadership, intellect, and courage, ensuring their inclusion in governance and security systems.

Part Two

Let's move forward to the climactic and monumental episode of the Ramayana: **The Battle of Lanka**. This epic confrontation is a tale of valor, strategy, divine interventions, and the triumph of righteousness over evil.

Prelude to War

As Rama's army crossed the Rama Setu and reached Lanka, the Vanaras and demons prepared for a colossal battle. The golden city of Lanka buzzed with tension as Ravana marshaled his forces, determined to defend his kingdom and retain Sita.

Meanwhile, Rama gathered his commanders Sugriva, Hanuman, Angada, and Jambavan and laid out his strategy. His plan emphasized discipline, teamwork, and minimizing unnecessary destruction. Rama's sole goal was to defeat Ravana, rescue Sita, and restore dharma.

Day One: The First Clash

The battle began with a thunderous roar as the Vanaras stormed the gates of Lanka. The demons, led by generals like Prahasta and Akampana, retaliated fiercely.

• **Hanuman's Strength:** Hanuman crushed entire battalions with his immense strength, leaping across the battlefield and hurling boulders at the enemy.

• **Angada's Valor:** Angada engaged in a duel with Ravana's son, Devantaka, defeating him with a single, powerful blow.

As the sun set, the first day ended with heavy losses on both sides. The Vanaras held their ground, but

Ravana's forces were relentless, and the war promised to intensify.

Day Two: The Sons of Ravana

Ravana sent his sons to challenge Rama's army.

- **Indrajit's Sorcery:** Ravana's most powerful son, Indrajit, wielded his mastery of illusion and summoned supernatural weapons. He cast a spell that rendered him invisible, raining fiery arrows upon Rama and Lakshmana.

- **During the war:** Lakshmana was injured by Indrajit; Hanuman had to intervene. And Lakshmana regained consciousness. Lakshmana countered with his exceptional archery, breaking Indrajit's spell and wounding him. However, Indrajit escaped, vowing to return stronger.

By dusk, the battlefield was soaked in blood, but Rama's army continued to push forward.

Day Three: Kumbhakarna Awakens

Realizing the strength of Rama's forces, Ravana summoned his colossal brother Kumbhakarna. A towering figure of immense power, Kumbhakarna struck terror into the hearts of the Vanaras as he stormed onto the battlefield, crushing soldiers underfoot.

- **Hanuman's Bravery:** Hanuman led the charge, attacking Kumbhakarna with mountain-sized boulders. Though fearless, Hanuman struggled to match the giant's raw power.

- **Rama's Victory:** Finally, Rama stepped forward, wielding his celestial weapons. With precision and divine strength, he severed Kumbhakarna's head, ending the demon's rampage and boosting the morale of his army.

The Turning Point: Indrajit's Last Stand

Determined to avenge his uncle, Indrajit returned to the battlefield with his deadliest weapon, the Nagapasha. This divine weapon unleashed venomous serpents that bound Rama and Lakshmana, rendering them immobile.

- **Garuda's Intervention:** As despair gripped the Vanaras, Garuda, the king of eagles and Rama's ally, descended from the heavens. His divine presence frightened the serpents, freeing Rama and Lakshmana from their binds.

Later, Lakshmana confronted Indrajit in a ferocious duel. Guided by Rama's blessings, Lakshmana struck Indrajit with a deadly arrow, finally ending the demon prince's life.

The Final Battle: Rama vs. Ravana

With his forces decimated, Ravana himself entered the battlefield. Clad in golden armor and wielding his fearsome weapons, he unleashed his fury upon the Vanara army.

- **Rama's Restraint:** Rama initially avoided killing Ravana, offering him a chance to surrender and return Sita. Ravana refused, consumed by arrogance and rage.

The battle between Rama and Ravana was a spectacle of divine power. The earth trembled as their celestial weapons clashed.

- **Ravana's Ten Heads:** Each time Rama severed one of Ravana's heads, it grew back, seemingly making him invincible.

The Brahmastra

Finally, Rama invoked the Brahmastra, a divine weapon imbued with the blessings of Brahma. Aiming it at Ravana's heart, Rama chanted sacred mantras and released the arrow.

The Brahmastra pierced Ravana's chest, destroying the source of his immortality and ending his reign of terror. As Ravana fell, the gods and sages of the heavens showered flowers upon Rama, praising the triumph of dharma.

Chapter Twenty Eight - Sita's Agni Pariksha

After the battle, Rama approached Sita, who had been anxiously waiting in the Ashoka Vatika. However, to uphold societal norms and dispel any doubts about her purity, Rama asked Sita to undergo the Agni Pariksha (trial by fire).

• **Sita's Faith:** Without hesitation, Sita stepped into the flames, her heart filled with unwavering trust in Rama. The fire god Agni emerged, declaring Sita's purity and returning her unharmed.

Rama embraced Sita, his mission complete. The couple, reunited at last, prepared to return to Ayodhya with their allies.

Significance of the Battle

1. **The Triumph of Dharma:** Rama's victory over Ravana symbolizes the ultimate triumph of good over evil.

2. **Unity and Sacrifice:** The battle highlights the importance of teamwork, sacrifice, and the strength of alliances in achieving a just cause.

3. **The Complexity of Rama's Character:** Rama's adherence to duty, even at the cost of personal pain, reflects his role as an ideal king and upholder of dharma.

Let's move to the joyous yet reflective Summary of the Ramayana: **Rama's Return to Ayodhya and His Coronation**. This chapter marks the culmination of Rama's exile, the fulfillment of his destiny, and his establishment as the ideal king of Ayodhya.

Chapter Twenty Nine - The Journey Back: Rama's Return to Ayodhya

Rama Bids Farewell to Lanka

After Ravana's defeat and Sita's reunion with Rama, preparations began for their return to Ayodhya. Bibhishan, Ravana's righteous brother who had allied with Rama, was crowned the new king of Lanka. He vowed to rule justly and remain a devoted ally of Rama.

Before leaving, Rama blessed the citizens of Lanka and thanked Bibhisan and the Vanaras for their support.

The Pushpaka Vimana

To expedite their journey back, Bibhishan offered Rama the Pushpaka Vimana, a celestial flying chariot originally crafted by Vishwakarma and seized by Ravana. Rama accepted and invited Lakshmana, Sita, Hanuman, and the Vanara chiefs to join him on this remarkable journey.

As the Pushpaka Vimana soared across the skies, Rama pointed out the various locations they had traversed during their exile, recounting their hardships and victories.

Hanuman's Mission to Ayodhya

Before reaching Ayodhya, Rama sent Hanuman ahead to inform Bharata of their return. Rama was aware of

Bharata's unwavering devotion and feared his brother might harm himself if he mistook any delay for bad news.

When Hanuman reached Nandigram, he found Bharata living like a hermit, dressed in bark and matted hair, awaiting Rama's return with a heart full of longing. Bharata wept tears of joy upon hearing the news and ordered preparations to welcome Rama with grandeur.

The Grand Homecoming

Ayodhya Rejoices

News of Rama's return spread like wildfire across Ayodhya. The streets were decorated with flowers, lamps, and colorful banners. Citizens thronged to the outskirts of the city, eager to catch a glimpse of their beloved prince.

When the Pushpaka Vimana descended, the air was filled with chants of "Jai Shri Ram!" Bharata, Shatrughna, and the royal family rushed forward to embrace Rama, Lakshmana, and Sita.

Bharata's Devotion

Bharata placed Rama's sandals, which he had preserved on the throne during his brother's exile, at Rama's feet. Falling to the ground, he said, "Ayodhya is yours once again, my Lord. I have merely been its caretaker."

Rama lifted Bharata and embraced him, praising his loyalty and sacrifice. The reunion of the brothers brought tears to everyone's eyes.

Chapter Thirty - The Coronation of Rama

Preparations for the Ceremony

The sages Vashistha, Vishwamitra, and others oversaw the arrangements for Rama's coronation. The people of Ayodhya prepared offerings and adorned the city in golden hues.

Rama, accompanied by Sita, entered the royal palace and greeted his mothers: Kaushalya, Kaikeyi, and Sumitra. Kaikeyi, filled with remorse, begged for Rama's forgiveness, and he reassured her with love and respect.

The Pattabhisheka

On the appointed day, Rama was crowned as the king of Ayodhya in a grand ceremony. Sita was glowing with grace sat by his side as the queen.

- **Divine Blessings:** Devas, sages, and celestial beings attended the coronation, showering blessings upon Rama and Sita.

- **Hanuman's Honor:** Hanuman, ever the humble devotee, stood by Rama's side, receiving special recognition for his unparalleled devotion and service.

Rama vowed to rule Ayodhya with fairness, compassion, and adherence to dharma, embodying the ideals of a perfect monarch.

The Golden Age: Rama Rajya

An Era of Prosperity

Rama's reign, known as Rama Rajya, became synonymous with justice, peace, and prosperity. Under his rule:

- The citizens of Ayodhya lived harmoniously, free from fear or want.

- The principles of dharma guided every aspect of governance.

- Nature flourished, and there was abundance everywhere.

Rama's Humility

Despite being a king, Rama remained humble and accessible to his people. He often walked among his citizens, listening to their concerns and ensuring their well-being. His commitment to dharma made him not just a ruler but a father figure to his people.

Reflections on Rama's Journey

Rama's return and coronation marked the end of a long journey filled with trials, sacrifices, and moral dilemmas. It symbolized the restoration of dharma and the triumph of good over evil.

1. **Brotherly Bonds:** The unwavering loyalty among Rama, Bharata, Lakshmana, and Shatrughna exemplified the ideal familial relationship.

2.   **Rama's Leadership:** His ability to inspire trust, unite diverse allies, and make difficult decisions showcased the qualities of a true leader.

3.   **Sita's Grace:** Sita's strength and resilience added depth to the narrative, reminding us of the quiet power of perseverance and faith.

Chapter Thirty One – Sita's Second Exile

Another exile

The coronation was not just the end of Rama's exile but the beginning of a golden era. However, the challenges of kingship would soon test Rama again, leading to events such as Sita's second exile and the birth of Lava and Kusha.

Let us continue with the bittersweet and contemplative later chapters of Rama's reign, focusing on **Sita's Second Exile and the Birth of Lava and Kusha**. This section reveals the complexities of Rama's role as a king and his unwavering commitment to dharma, even at great personal cost.

The Shadow of Doubt

Despite the joyous beginning of Rama Rajya, whispers of doubt about Sita's purity began circulating among the citizens of Ayodhya. Some questioned whether Sita, who had spent time in Ravana's captivity, could be accepted as the queen of Ayodhya.

Though Sita's Agni Pariksha had proven her chastity, Rama was deeply troubled by the unrest among his people. As an ideal king, he prioritized the welfare and trust of his subjects over his personal happiness.

The Heartbreaking Decision

Rama summoned his trusted brother Lakshmana and revealed his decision to send Sita away. He said, "A king's duty is to uphold the faith of his people. Though my heart breaks, I must distance myself from Sita to preserve the integrity of my rule."

Lakshmana, shocked and devastated, pleaded with Rama to reconsider, but Rama remained firm in his resolve.

Sita's Exile

The Journey to Valmiki's Ashram

With a heavy heart, Lakshmana escorted a pregnant Sita to the forest. Unaware of Rama's decision, Sita assumed they were going on a pilgrimage. However, as they reached the outskirts of the forest, Lakshmana tearfully explained Rama's command.

Sita was struck with grief but displayed immense dignity. She said, "If this is my Lord's wish, I shall obey without question. May my children be born in purity, and may they bring glory to Rama's name."

Lakshmana left Sita at the hermitage of Sage Valmiki, where she found solace and protection. Valmiki welcomed her with compassion, understanding the weight of her sorrow.

The Birth of Lava and Kusha

In Valmiki's ashram, Sita gave birth to twin sons, Lava and Kusha. The boys were raised in the serene environment of the forest, learning the values of dharma, courage, and humility.

Their Education

Under Valmiki's guidance, Lava and Kusha became proficient in:

•   **Vedas and Scriptures:** They mastered sacred texts, embodying the wisdom of their lineage.

•   **Martial Arts:** They trained in archery and swordsmanship, inheriting the warrior skills of their father.

•   **Music and Poetry:** The twins also learned to sing and play instruments, excelling in the recital of the Ramayana, which Valmiki had composed.

Sita, despite her sorrow, found joy in raising her sons, ensuring they grew into virtuous and capable young men.

Chapter Thirty Two - Rama Meets Lava and Kusha and aftermath

The Ashvamedha Yajna

Years later, Rama decided to perform the Ashvamedha Yajna to affirm his sovereignty and bring prosperity to Ayodhya. As per tradition, a sacrificial horse was released to roam freely, challenging any kingdom that tried to capture it.

The horse wandered near Valmiki's ashram, where Lava and Kusha, unaware of their lineage, stopped it. They considered it their duty to protect their territory and engaged in combat with Rama's army.

The Duel

Rama's generals were astonished by the twins' skill and valor. Even Lakshmana found himself overpowered by the young warriors. Eventually, Rama himself arrived to face them.

As Rama engaged in combat, he was struck by the boys' resemblance to himself. Their mannerisms, courage, and mastery of weapons revealed their heritage.

The Reunion

Sage Valmiki intervened, bringing Sita to the battlefield. He revealed the truth about Lava and

Kusha's parentage, declaring them the rightful heirs of Ayodhya.

Sita, filled with emotion, introduced her sons to Rama. However, she also expressed her pain and the injustice she had endured.

Sita's Final Plea

Sita turned to the earth, her eternal mother, and said, 'If I have been pure and faithful, may the earth accept me and provide me peace.'

In a miraculous moment, the ground opened, and Sita was embraced by Mother Earth. She disappeared into the earth, leaving Rama and her sons in profound grief.

The Legacy of Lava and Kusha

Though devastated by Sita's departure, Rama welcomed Lava and Kusha into the royal household. He ensured they were educated and prepared to lead Ayodhya with wisdom and justice.

The twins grew into exemplary leaders, upholding the legacy of their parents. Their rule symbolized the continuation of dharma and the values instilled in them by Sita and Valmiki.

Rama's Departure

Years later, when Rama's time on earth came to an end, he handed over the kingdom to Lava and Kusha. Accompanied by his loyal brothers, Rama walked into the Sarayu River, merging with his divine essence as Vishnu.

Themes and Reflections

1.   **Sita's Strength:** Sita's unwavering grace and resilience, even in the face of adversity, make her one of the most dignified characters in Indian mythology.

2.   **Rama's Dilemma:** His decision to exile Sita highlights the complex interplay between personal emotions and public duty.

3.   **Lava and Kusha's Legacy:** The twins embody the promise of a brighter future, carrying forward the values of dharma and justice.

Let us delve into **the philosophical interpretations** of these profound events in the Ramayana. These moments: Sita's exile, the upbringing of Lava and Kusha, and the eventual reunion and separation: carry deep lessons on dharma, morality, and human relationships.

Chapter Thirty Three - Critical Analysis of some events

Sita's Exile; The Burden of Dharma

Rama's Dilemma as King and Husband

Rama's decision to exile Sita reflects the eternal conflict between personal love and public duty. As a king, Rama prioritized the trust and satisfaction of his subjects, even at the expense of his own happiness.

Philosophical Perspective:

• Dharma vs. Adharma: The story illustrates the complexities of dharma. While Rama upheld the dharma of kingship, his decision might seem unjust to Sita on a personal level, raising questions about whether adhering to societal expectations always serves the greater good.

• Ideal vs. Real: Rama, often seen as the ideal man, is portrayed here in a deeply human light. His anguish shows the difficulty of making decisions when bound by conflicting duties.

Sita's Strength in Adversity

Despite being wronged, Sita displayed dignity and unwavering faith in Rama and her own purity. Her willingness to accept exile reflects inner strength and grace.

Philosophical Perspective:

•	Faith in Justice: Sita's life teaches an importance of maintaining faith in truth and justice, even when circumstances seem unfair.

•	The Feminine Ideal: Her journey represents the resilience of women who endure and rise above societal judgment.

The Upbringing of Lava and Kusha: A Reflection on Parenting

Sita as a Mother

Sita's focus on raising Lava and Kusha with strong moral values highlights the role of parenting in shaping future generations. Despite her isolation and sorrow, she ensured that her sons were educated in dharma, valor, and compassion.

Philosophical Perspective:

•	Nurturing Values: The story underscores the importance of a mother's role in instilling virtues that transcend personal grief or circumstances.

•	Legacy of Dharma: Lava and Kusha symbolize hope, showing how the principles of dharma can be passed down and sustained through proper guidance.

The Ashvamedha Yajna: Symbolism of Conflict and Reunion

The Battle with Lava and Kusha

The conflict between Rama and his sons during the Ashvamedha Yajna symbolizes ignorance giving way to revelation. Neither side knew their true connection, yet they fought valiantly, only to be reunited by Valmiki's intervention.

Philosophical Perspective:

• Karma's Unfolding: The battle signifies how karma unfolds in mysterious ways, bringing people together or creating conflict based on past actions.

• Unity beyond Division: The reunion highlights that truth ultimately dissolves misunderstandings and restores harmony.

Sita's Return to Mother Earth: Liberation and Justice

Sita's Final Act

By returning to her mother, the Earth, Sita symbolically transcended worldly judgment. Her departure can be seen as an act of liberation and a rejection of societal constraints.

Philosophical Perspective:

• Returning to the Source: Sita's return signifies the cyclical nature of existence. She came from the Earth and returned to it, symbolizing detachment from material bonds.

• Justice in Nature: While human society doubted her, nature: the ultimate witness: acknowledged her purity and provided her solace.

Rama's Reign and Departure: The End of Dharma's Cycle

The Legacy of Rama Rajya

Rama's reign represented the ideal of dharma, where governance was based on justice, compassion, and adherence to truth. However, his personal sacrifices show the cost of upholding such ideals.

Philosophical Perspective:

• Ideal Leadership: Rama's reign reminds us that true leadership requires prioritizing collective welfare over individual desires.

• The Inescapable Cycle: Rama's departure into the Sarayu River signifies the transient nature of human roles, even those of divine beings. Every cycle, no matter how perfect, must come to an end.

Key Themes for Reflection

1. **The Relativity of Dharma:** Dharma is not absolute; it must adapt to circumstances. Rama and Sita's lives illustrate the difficulty of choosing the greater good over personal happiness.

2. **Strength in Adversity:** Sita's character shows how one can endure injustice with grace and leave behind a legacy of hope and righteousness.

3. **Unity of the Divine and Human:** Despite their divine origins, Rama and Sita's struggles reflect human emotions and challenges, making them relatable and inspiring.

4. **Cycles of Karma:** The Ramayana demonstrates how karma manifests across generations, shaping relationships and destinies in unexpected ways.

Philosophical Questions to Ponder

•	Was Rama's decision to exile Sita truly dharmic, or did it expose the flaws in societal expectations of leadership?

•	How does Sita's return to the Earth redefine justice in the context of divine intervention?

•	Could the ideals of Rama Rajya exist in today's world, and what sacrifices would be required to achieve it?

Chapter Thirty Four - Thematic conceptualization with contemporary relevance

Let's continue exploring the philosophical and thematic depths of the Ramayana. This time, we will focus on **specific lessons drawn from pivotal events** and **their relevance to contemporary life**. Each section will highlight the universality of the epic's wisdom and how it resonates across cultures and eras.

The Balance of Personal and Public Duty

Rama's Sacrifices

Rama's life is marked by decisions that prioritize the greater good over personal desires: be it his decision to accept exile, his abandonment of Sita, or his embrace of a lonely kingship. Each choice underscores the tension between personal happiness and the responsibilities of leadership.

Contemporary Relevance:

•	Work-Life Balance: Modern leaders and individuals often face the challenge of balancing professional obligations with personal well-being. Rama's story invites reflection on when and how to prioritize collective welfare while acknowledging personal costs.

- Ethical Governance: Rama's adherence to dharma shows the importance of integrity and selflessness in leadership, qualities still relevant in political and corporate domains.

Philosophical Question:

Can a leader truly serve the public without sacrificing personal desires? If so, how can they find fulfillment?

The Role of Women in Society: Sita's Grace and Strength

Sita's Journey

Sita's trials: her abduction, the Agni Pariksha, and her eventual exile; highlight the societal expectations placed on women. Despite this, Sita remains steadfast in her dignity, strength, and devotion.

Contemporary Relevance:

- Breaking Stereotypes: Sita's unwavering strength amidst adversity challenges the misconception of her as merely submissive. She is a figure of resilience, representing the potential for women to rise above societal judgment.

- Equality and Respect: The Ramayana invites us to question and reshape societal norms to ensure respect and equality for women in all spheres of life.

Philosophical Question:

How can we reinterpret ancient stories like the Ramayana to empower women in modern times without losing their essence?

Forgiveness and Reconciliation: The Episode of Shabari

Shabari's Devotion

Shabari, a tribal woman, waits her entire life to serve Rama and offers him fruits, tasting each to ensure they are sweet. Rama accepts her offering with gratitude, transcending caste and societal prejudices.

Contemporary Relevance:

• Breaking Barriers: The story underscores the importance of inclusivity and dismantling social hierarchies. It shows that true devotion and goodness transcend external identities.

• Compassion in Action: Rama's acceptance of Shabari's offering teaches us to recognize and value sincerity over superficial norms.

Philosophical Question:

In a world divided by class, race, and religion, how can we embody the universal compassion exemplified by Rama?

The Nature of Justice: Ravana's Redemption

Ravana's Complex Character

Ravana is a learned scholar, a devotee of Shiva, and a capable ruler. His downfall lies in his arrogance and inability to control his desires. Despite his flaws, Rama ensures that Ravana receives a dignified death, acknowledging his virtues.

Contemporary Relevance:

- Restorative Justice: Rather than demonizing adversaries, the Ramayana advocates understanding their virtues and offering redemption. This approach aligns with modern ideas of restorative justice, which seeks to heal rather than punish.

- Acknowledging Complexity: Ravana's character reminds us that even those we oppose have redeeming qualities, encouraging empathy and understanding.

Philosophical Question:

How can societies balance justice with compassion, especially when dealing with adversaries or wrongdoers?

The Power of Education: Lava and Kusha's Upbringing

Valmiki's Mentorship

The education of Lava and Kusha under Valmiki's guidance showcases the transformative power of learning. They inherit the best of their lineage: Rama's valor and Sita's virtue, through rigorous training and moral instruction.

Contemporary Relevance:

- Holistic Education: The emphasis on combining spiritual wisdom, martial skills, and the arts highlights the importance of well-rounded education.

- Role of Mentors: Valmiki's role as a guide reflects the critical impact of mentors in shaping young minds.

Philosophical Question:

In an age dominated by specialization, how can we cultivate holistic learning that balances intellect, morality, and creativity?

The Cycle of Karma: Sita's Return to the Earth

Sita's Final Act

Sita's return to the Earth signifies her liberation from worldly trials and the culmination of her journey of dharma. Her act reaffirms the idea of returning to one's source and the impermanence of material life.

Contemporary Relevance:

•	Detachment and Liberation: In a world obsessed with material success, Sita's story encourages detachment and a focus on inner peace.

•	Justice Beyond Humans: Her return to the Earth symbolizes nature's ultimate authority and the inevitability of divine justice.

Philosophical Question:

How can we reconcile the pursuit of worldly success with the spiritual quest for liberation?

Unity and Brotherhood: Rama and His Allies

The Bonds of Friendship

From Hanuman's unwavering devotion to Sugriva's alliance and Lakshmana's sacrifices, the Ramayana highlights the strength of unity and the value of selfless relationships.

Contemporary Relevance:

•   Collaboration over Competition: The unity of Rama's allies serves as a model for teamwork and collective action, especially in solving complex challenges.

•   The Role of Allies in Success: The Ramayana teaches us to value and nurture's meaningful relationships, recognizing that success is rarely a solo journey.

Philosophical Question:

In an increasingly individualistic world, how can we foster genuine connections and collaborative efforts?

Themes for Reflection and Action

1.   **Dharma in Complexity:** Life often presents conflicting duties, and the Ramayana encourages thoughtful deliberation and courage in decision-making.

2.   **Empathy across Divides:** The stories of Shabari and Ravana remind us of the transformative power of empathy and inclusion.

3.   **The Legacy of Learning:** Lava and Kusha's upbringing underscores the lifelong impact of mentors and education.

4.   **Justice with Compassion:** Rama's treatment of allies and adversaries alike shows that true justice involves dignity and understanding.

Epilogue

1. Social Perspective: Unity in Diversity

- ### Hierarchy and Duty:

In ancient Indian society, the Varna system defined roles and responsibilities. The Ramayana reflects this, with Kshatriyas like Rama adhering to their duty as warriors and rulers. However, the epic also critiques the rigidity of this system. Shabari, a tribal woman, is elevated through her devotion, challenging societal hierarchies. Similarly, Jatayu, a bird, becomes a hero by sacrificing his life for Sita, demonstrating that social standing does not determine virtue.

- ### Inclusion of Marginalized Groups:

Rama's acceptance of Guha, a tribal king, as an equal ally, and Hanuman's prominent role, despite being a Vanara, highlight the epic's inclusive ethos. These relationships promote the idea that virtue and loyalty transcend caste and species.

- ### Community Values:

The people of Ayodhya play an active role in the epic, voicing concerns about their king's actions. This reflects the democratic underpinnings of ancient governance, where rulers were accountable to their subjects. The exile of Sita, though morally contentious, was driven by Rama's commitment to upholding societal expectations

2. Cultural Perspective: Preservation and Adaptation

- **Festivals and Rituals:**

The Ramayana immortalizes rituals like the Ashwamedha Yajna, symbolizing sovereignty and divine approval for kingship. Rama's coronation is a grand cultural celebration, uniting people across social strata, emphasizing shared cultural heritage.

- **Intercultural Exchange:**

The epic's geographic span from Ayodhya to Lanka; illustrates a rich tapestry of cultural diversity. Ayodhya's refined culture contrasts with the opulence and advanced architecture of Ravana's Lanka. This contrast serves as a metaphor for the coexistence of moral righteousness (Ayodhya) and material grandeur (Lanka).

- **Art and Literature:**

Ravana, a polymath, composed the Shiva Tandava Stotram and created the Ravana Vina. These contributions underscore how even morally flawed characters can enrich cultural and artistic traditions.

3. Structural Perspective: Dharma as the Foundation

- **Governance:**

Rama epitomizes the concept of Rama Rajya, an ideal state where the ruler prioritizes justice, fairness, and the welfare of his subjects. This model of governance balances personal desires and public responsibilities, offering a timeless ideal for ethical leadership.

- **Family Dynamics:**

The Ramayana portrays family as a microcosm of society. The bond between Dasharatha and Rama illustrates the interplay of love and duty, while Kaikeyi's actions demonstrate how individual desires can disrupt familial harmony. Yet, Bharata's refusal to ascend the throne reflects selflessness, underscoring the resilience of familial bonds.

- **Allied Forces:**

Rama's coalition with the Vanaras, including leaders like Sugriva and Hanuman, demonstrates the effectiveness of decentralized leadership. This alliance reflects the power of cooperation, where diverse entities unite under a shared goal.

4. Relational Perspective: Bonds beyond Blood

- **Friendships:**

The friendship between Rama and Sugriva illustrates mutual trust. Sugriva regains his throne with Rama's help, while Sugriva's army aids Rama in rescuing Sita. Similarly, Hanuman's devotion transcends loyalty, embodying spiritual surrender.

- **Brotherhood:**

Lakshmana's unwavering support for Rama, even in exile, contrasts with Bharata's anguish over inheriting the throne. Shatrughna's quiet dedication highlights the spectrum of brotherly virtues, from selflessness to silent sacrifice.

- **Spousal Relationships:**

Rama and Sita's bond reflects ideals of love, trust, and shared values. Their separation tests their resilience, emphasizing the strength of their spiritual connection. Conversely, Ravana's treatment of Mandodari shows the consequences of neglecting mutual respect in marriage.

5. Personal Perspective: Growth through Adversity

- **Rama's Evolution:**

Rama's exile is a transformative journey. Initially bound by royal expectations, he grows into a spiritually awakened leader. The challenges he faces teach him resilience, empathy, and the true meaning of dharma.

- **Sita's Strength:**

Sita's endurance during her abduction by Ravana exemplifies inner strength and dignity. Her refusal to yield to Ravana's advances underscores her unwavering faith and moral fortitude, inspiring generations of women.

- **Ravana's Complexity:**

Ravana's brilliance as a scholar and his flaws as a ruler reflect the duality of human nature. His fall serves as a cautionary tale about the perils of unchecked ambition and ego, highlighting the importance of self-awareness.

6. Ethical Perspective: Moral Dilemmas and Their Lessons

- **Dharma vs. Adharma:**

Rama's decisions often pit personal desires against societal expectations. His exile of Sita, while controversial, underscores the ethical complexity of dharma, where personal sacrifice is often required to uphold social harmony.

- **Justice and Mercy:**

Bibhishan's acceptance into Rama's fold, despite being Ravana's brother, highlights Rama's commitment to justice. This act demonstrates the importance of judging individuals by their actions rather than their associations.

- **Accountability:**

Kaikeyi's eventual remorse for her actions reflects the theme of accountability. Her journey from ambition to repentance underscores the possibility of redemption through self-reflection.

7. Moral Perspective: Principles over Expediency

- **Truth and Righteousness:**

Rama's commitment to fulfilling his father's promise, even at great personal cost, exemplifies the moral principle of truthfulness. This unwavering adherence to dharma reinforces the importance of integrity in leadership.

- **Service and Sacrifice:**

Lakshmana's willingness to forsake comforts for Rama, and Hanuman's tireless efforts to serve him, highlight the moral value of selflessness and dedication.

- **Consequences of Actions:**

Ravana's downfall, driven by his ethical lapses, serves as a moral lesson on the inevitability of justice. Conversely, Rama's triumph illustrates the rewards of steadfast virtue.

8. Spiritual Perspective: Journey to Liberation

- **Divine Manifestation:**

Rama as an avatar of Vishnu symbolizes the cosmic balance between good and evil. His journey represents the divine interplay of fate and free will, offering spiritual lessons for humanity.

- **Path to Moksha:**

Hanuman embodies devotion (Bhakti), while Rama exemplifies righteous action (karma). Together, they offer complementary paths to liberation, emphasizing the universality of spiritual ideals.

- **Universal Message:**

The Ramayana's overarching theme the triumph of good over evil resonates universally, emphasizing faith, perseverance, and divine grace as tools for overcoming life's challenges.

The Ramayana is more than an epic; it is a profound exploration of human and cosmic relationships. Each perspective social, cultural, structural, relational, personal, ethical, moral, and spiritual offers valuable insights into navigating life's complexities. By addressing universal themes through timeless narratives, the Ramayana remains a cornerstone of ethical, spiritual, and philosophical discourse. Its characters, dilemmas, and lessons continue to inspire humanity, bridging the gap between ancient wisdom and contemporary relevance.

About the Author

Aurobindo Ghosh

Dr. Aurobindo Ghosh belongs to a renowned Mahashayjee family of Bhagalpur. His multifaceted talent was visible in his early age. In academic field, he completed his M.Sc, M.Phil, Ph.D in Statistics, Ph.D in Economics. As a college professor, he was always in demand. In social field, his contribution to the society is unparallel. He collected quite a few Good Samaritan to perform marriage to quite a few poor marriageable girls in Amravati, Maharashtra. His linguistic ability is notable. He can speak, read and write in Bengali, Hindi, Marathi, Bhagalpuri, English, and Gujarati with ease. His passion for writing in various languages resulted in many solos and anthologies. Notable amongst them are Lily on the Northern Sky (Awarded by Ukiyoto), Insight Outsight (A collection of short stories), Mejoder Golpo (Bengali short story collection), Chhondo Hole Mondo Ki (Bengali Poems), Bimladadi's Dream (Awarded by Ukiyoto), Mystical Honeymoon, and Deception Redefined. Recently he has introduced his detective character Suborno Deb Barman through his trilogy,

"Mysteries of Suborno Deb barman (14 crime stories), Chronicles of Suborno Deb Barman (Six crime stories) and Chronicles of Suborno Deb Barman-Mystery of stolen memory". His short stories and poems in different languages are included in more than twenty anthologies. Many of his books are translated in various international languages such as German, Italian, Spanish, Turkish, French, and Nepali and so on. He is also an artist of high caliber. He is expert in Madhubani and Warli painting. His acrylic abstracts are appreciated a lot. He is a traveler who travels around the globe. Recently he has shifted his attention towards Mythological research in Indian context. His critical analytical book on Mahabharata is coming soon. This present book on Ramayana is the natural extension of the first one.

www.ingramcontent.com/pod-product-compliance
Lightning Source LLC
LaVergne TN
LVHW091658190726
843493LV00001B/53